an A... Schoolboy

'...ry funny . . . lots of jokes about perfectly ordinary things we ... but if you view it from an alien's point of view, they look ...rfectly ridiculous. Very good fun to read and the illustrations ...e fantastic.'
...he Guardian

'...e humour is infectiously funny, and more importantly relevant. ... relevant, that it has genuine deeper undertones on diversity – ...-diversity, equality, acceptance, historical meaning, lessons ...nt and the danger of not learning them. It is like reading a ...d's version of Douglas Adams's *Hitchhiker's Guide to the* ...xy.'
...e Away

'... of this world. Endlessly inventive . . . will tickle and touch ...ren's imagination.'
...Vhybrow, author of *Harry and the Bucketful of Dinosaurs*

'Very different and very funny. You will see our very comical world quite differently.'
Jeremy Strong

'Imagine *My Step Parents Are Aliens* ...ing with *The Secret Diary of Adrian Mole*. ...at laugh.'
...usel

'...rrific series for both boys and girls. Packed with hilarious ...trations – a real page-turner.'
...eading4kids

Ros Asquith started out as a photographer, became a theatre critic for *Time Out*, *City Limits*, and *The Observer* before emerging as a cartoonist. She draws regularly for *The Guardian* and has written and illustrated many books.

Ros lives in London with her jazz critic husband and two sons. She has stroked a tiger, cuddled a wolf, caught an escaped tarantula and juggled in a circus, but mostly prefers reading and eating fudge.

Find out more at www.rosasquith.co.uk

Discover what happened on Flowkwee's first trip to Earth!

LETTERS from an ALIEN SCHOOLBOY
Cosmic Custard

*Translated from Alien
by Professor R.L. Asquith*

Piccadilly Press • London

★

TO LOLA BRUCE

*and with big thanks to
my lovely editor Ruth Williams,
my lovely husband John Fordham
and my dear agent Rosemary Canter*

★

First published in Great Britain in 2011 by
Piccadilly Press Ltd, 5 Castle Road, London NW1 8PR
www.piccadillypress.co.uk

Cover and text designed by Simon Davis

ISBN: 978 1 84812 149 2
1 3 5 7 9 10 8 6 4 2

Printed and bound by CPI Group (UK) Ltd, Croydon, CR0 4YY

Cosmic Custard

Earthlings are hopeless duffers who cannot balance a ball on their beaks like the friendly seal, or open a packet of 'crisps' without them exploding.

BUT FEAR NOT!

The grown-up ones are about to be Improved. Get your aunties, dads, uncles, mums, teachers, grannies and grandpas to follow the instructions on our magnificent Improver – a fiendish machine that civilises Earthlings – and they will be Improved beyond their wildest dreams. This means you, my friendly reader, will be allowed to stay up all night eating sweeties.

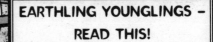

**EARTHLING YOUNGLINGS –
READ THIS!**

Get ALL the grown-ups to follow this sign.
Then they will be IMPROVED so YOU will
have ICE CREAM, free video games,
FOOTBALL PITCHES on every street,
and all the sweets you can eat.

FREE HEALTH CLUB *AND* BEAUTY PARLOUR
LOSE WEIGHT GET FIT

(As well as Peace on Earth
and any pet you want including rats.)

MISSION EARTH TWO:
DAY ONE - THURSDAY

Same Old Measly Dwelling
Row of Identical Dwellings
Titchy 'Country' Called England
Insignificant Blob Called Earth
Small, Dim Solar System
Forty-third Galaxy from the Right
Virgo Supercluster
Still at the Wrong End of the Universe

But at least
we're no longer
inside cell 9000,
vilest prison in
Universe.

Dear Rok,

Bad news – we're not coming home to Planet Faa
yet. I was longing to wrap seven tentacles around all
my mums and dads again. And I couldn't wait to see
you, my dear old friend.

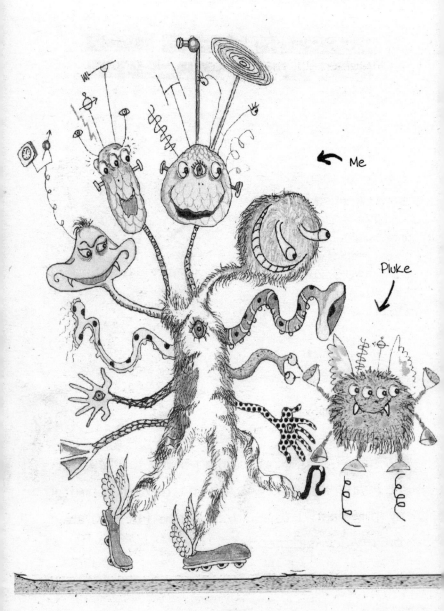

Me

Pluke

I imagined this magical scene.

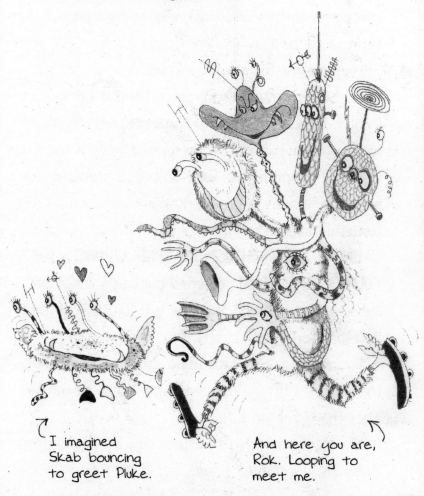

I imagined
Skab bouncing
to greet Pluke.

And here you are,
Rok. Looping to
meet me.

Instead, we're back on the freezing, grumpy old spaceblob Earth – the *flarrmsnaarg* ('armpit' is the Earth word for it) of the Universe.

Here are the full horrible details.

Flyzoop, the Worst Pilot Since The Big Bang, was flying our spaceship back to Faa at well over the three kazillion lightyears-per-second speed limit, as usual. I was just hoping we wouldn't get stopped for speeding when the in-flight panic signal told us something was wrong.

'ENEMY APPROACHING! REVERSE AT ONCE INTO FOURTH DIMENSION!' bleeped our trusty robot *Bertiolboomflinglebuntusdyoliusfloopfloop*. (I just call him Bert for short.)

Flyzoop lost his heads as soon as he heard Bert. He flung up his suckers, whimpering, 'I surrender. They made me do it.'

The door imploded and six savage *barflesplurgers*, dribbling luminous slime, burst in followed by

Barflesplurger (this one is pictured in a gentle mood. His name is Spot)

customs officials pointing those weapons that can vaporise all four of your heads at once.

'Citizens of Faa!' snarled the chief. 'You are a disgrace to the name of his Holy-roly-poliness the Emperor. You have betrayed his mighty cause and landed yourselves in the soup.'

My sister Farteeta and me hid behind Bert, pulling Susan with us. Susan is my Earthling friend who we were bringing back to Faa.

'We have reason to believe you have an illegal Earthling on board.' The chief spotted Susan cowering behind Bert and yanked her out. 'Hah! Just as we thought – a puny specimen. The worst kind too – from England,' he muttered, holding his nationality-scanner at full tentacle length, as though Susan was infectious. Then he spoke to her in perfect English. 'Where are your documents?'

Susan emptied her 'pockets' (peculiar pouches Earthlings use to carry their important stuff) but there was no intergalactic passport in there.

The chief used all his four heads to snuffle the

'Paperclip'
for joining one
bit of paper to
another bit of
paper.

'Fluff' Important item in
all Earthling pockets. I
am as yet uncertain of
its use, but either they
believe it is lucky or
else it is a medicine.

'Bogey tissues'
Sorry, Rok, but in
the interests of
science I must
expose you to
these unsavoury
items.

Chocolate 'sweetie'

'Key' Earthlings have
to lock their houses
every time they go
out, in case other
Earthlings steal their
paperclips.

'Money'
Earthlings love
this best of all

INSIDE SUSAN's 'Pocket'

chocolate, making slurping noises like an Earthling at lunch.

SLURP SLURP BELCH

'Anyway, you're all nicked, me old *flackersnicks*,' he said when he'd finished.

'We can sort this out,' said Papa, drawing himself up to his full eight metres. 'The Earthling is just accompanying us home to Faa for a short visit —'

'SILENCE when you speak to an Imperial Officer,' the chief yelled. 'They all pretend it's a visit, then they steal our jobs and our homes and before you know it they're everywhere. It'll have to be deported.'

He turned to Susan. 'You are under arrest. I warn you that everything will be taken down and used in evidence, including your socks.'

'Will I be sent back to Earth?' asked Susan, happily.

'Punished first. Maybe we'll make you walk the plank into the well of despair, where there are no mobile phones or hairdryers. Unless you have more cocoa solids?'

But Susan didn't have any more chocolate so we were all bundled into a slimy prison cell on their spaceship.

Papa messaged home to explain the situation to the Secretive Services he works for, hoping they would tell the customs officials that we'd been on a secret mission. They were not pleased.

YOU HAVE CAUGHT ONE FEEBLE EARTHLING? YOUR MISSION WAS TO CAPTURE AND IMPROVE HUNDREDS OF EARTHLINGS FOR USE AS SLAVES ON FAA. RETURN TO EARTH IMMEDIATELY. HAIL TO THE EMPEROR.

'Shame, it would've been fun to make 'em walk the plank,' said the chief, shoving us back into our spaceship.

We dropped by the Helix Nebula's Happy-Snax

bar for *Vom* supplies (to stop our Earth disguises dissolving when we're 'stressed'). Then we shrank back to being Earthlings, with just one head, four useless limbs and only two eyeballs.

I have to be a schoolboy again, called Hoover Bogey Nigel Custard Toilet Hercules Namby Pamby Harmonica Hedgehog Coldplay Bugspray Cro-Magnon Colander Junior (Nigel Colander for short). And I have to pretend to have a brain that can't even price up the kids' menu at a fly-in *flaaark* branch, let alone begin to think about why time bends.

'It's nice to have you back as Nigel,' said Susan. 'You're really scary as Flowkweewee or whatever.'

I don't think she liked my four handsome heads, or my suckers.

Flyzoop dropped us off an hour after we'd first left Earth, using the space/time coordinates that Earthlings have no clue about. (They cannot do even the most basic time travel, not even a second forwards.)

'It's still Thursday,' said Susan. 'My mum won't even know I've been gone.'

Farteeta pointed the memory blaster at her. 'And neither will you.'

'That won't work now she's been out of Earth's atmosphere,' said Papa. 'What *do* they teach you in school? Anyway, no one will believe Susan if she says she's been in a spaceship with a bunch of four-headed aliens and a giant robot.'

So here we are, back in our wretched little Earth 'rooms' called 'bath' or 'bed'. Earthlings are fonder of their rooms than they are of their own children. They are always buying them presents of curtains (for shutting out moonlight) and carpets (to warm their floors) and complicated furnitures.

Remember how cold I said Earth was? Well, it's worse now. Mama is trying to light a warmer-upper with primitive twigs called 'matches'. She is rubbing them together like the Earthling warriors

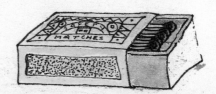

('boy scouts') do but it isn't working.

We have put on 'winter clothes' made from scratchy-furred Earth creatures called 'sheeps'. Imagine 'gloves' Rok – a woolly hat for each digit.

I liked these pink and violet <u>welly boots</u> but Susan said, no.

<u>'Glove'</u>

Hats for 'fingers'

Hat for 'thumb'

Rok, if you are ever forced into a 'jumper' wear one with an Earthling Hero on it, not a teddy. Earthling Heroes are men in tights named after superior creatures like bats or spiders.

<u>'Jumper'</u> a disappointing clothe. It does not jump but merely hangs about.

Me in my 'winter clothes'

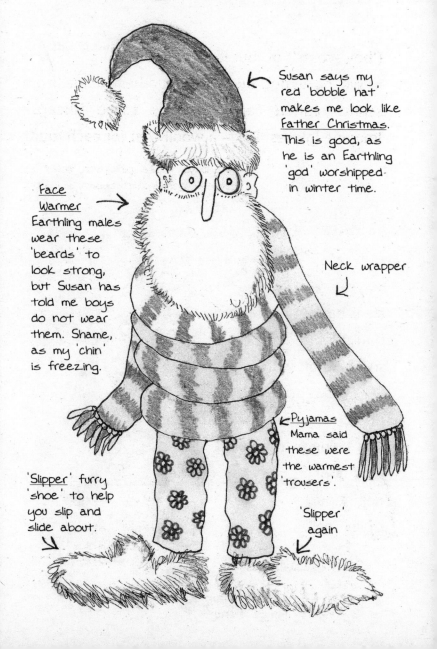

Susan says my red 'bobble hat' makes me look like <u>Father Christmas</u>. This is good, as he is an Earthling 'god' worshipped in winter time.

<u>Face Warmer</u>
Earthling males wear these 'beards' to look strong, but Susan has told me boys do not wear them. Shame, as my 'chin' is freezing.

Neck wrapper

<u>Pyjamas</u>
Mama said these were the warmest 'trousers'.

'<u>Slipper</u>' furry 'shoe' to help you slip and slide about.

'Slipper' again

At least Pluke is happy.

Pluke is so happy
because now he is . . .

ol Fi Fi my love

He is back in his Earth
dog disguise and
sneaking off with
Fi Fi, the repulsive
poodle creature
that belongs to my
next door
neighbour,
Colin Snell.

. . . Rhubarb again. And all he
can think of is running off
into the bushes with Fi Fi.

The Secretive Services sent Papa the Emperor's new orders:

CAPTURE AND IMPROVE ADULT EARTHLINGS AND BRING BACK ANIMAL SAMPLES TOO BEFORE ALL EARTH LIFE BECOMES EXTINCT. FAILURE WILL BE PUNISHED BY VAPORISATION. EFFICIENCY BREEDS CONTENT. HAIL TO THE EMPEROR.
By order, Pleefpyfleefpy,
Chief Assistant to the Assistant Chief

Then Papa turned to me and said these wonderful words, Rok, making my hearts glow with pride: 'Flowkwee, you proved yourself brave and true during the Thregg Invasion. I therefore put you in charge of collecting animal species. This will be *footlingly* easy compared to the hard work Bert and I will have, capturing and Improving Earthling adults. I can only imagine the Emperor has chosen adults this time because he hopes they may have more brain cells than pathetic Earthling children.'

'It's not fair,' said Farteeta. 'I helped defeat the Threggs as much as Flowkwee did. What's *my* Mission?'

'Girls don't have Missions, Farty.' Papa smiled and ruffled her hairstyle. 'Go and play with your Barby doll.'

Papa doesn't seem to have learnt that on Earth, females are almost as good as

IT'S NOT FAIR!

↑ Keith, King of Threggs

males, or that Farteeta has a brain that works quite like yours and mine.

It will be excellent finding creatures to bring home. My class are going on a school trip to a 'farm' next week, where Earthlings keep pet vegetables and animals, so I'll be able to capture some of the ones that I've read about in Earth books.

I have not found a picture of a <u>mermaid</u> yet, but I have heard that it is half 'fish', half female Earthling, so I expect it looks like this. I intend to capture one and free it from cold H_2O (which on Earth is called 'water').

I really want to find a <u>gorgon</u> they have beautiful frizzy hair and can turn Earthlings to *<u>stone</u> which could be very useful.

*'Stone' is a lazy name for multiple elements and minerals: carbon, selenium, silicon, iron, etc.

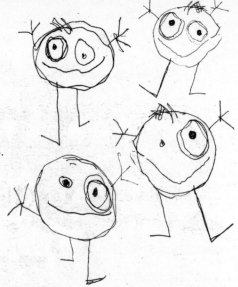

I must capture one of these. ⟶
All little children here draw them, so they must be popular pets.

'We have swimming at school tomorrow,' I told Farteeta. 'So I can hunt for a mermaid first.'

'I want a mermaid,' said Farteeta.

'You can get a "goldfish" from your playgroup tank,' I said. 'They also have lovely scales like us. Earthlings are very cruel to them, forcing them to live in water.'

'Good idea,' said Farteeta. 'We can release the goldfish into a nice field when we get home to Faa.'

'WERF WERF WERFETTY WERF.'

Pluke came bounding in whining, his horrid dog 'tail' between his legs.

'Whatever's the matter, Pluke?' I asked him.

'They have stolen my puppies and put them in a cage,' he said sadly.

Poor Pluke. Remember the nice two-headed puppies that he had with Fi Fi? Apparently Colin's papa has sold them to an animal museum called a 'zoo' to be investigated.

'Don't worry, Pluke, we will rescue them,' was all I could think of saying.

He kept on whining so I agreed to read him a story, to help him sleep. You know Pluke likes to be frightened at bedtime, so I chose Bert's *Encyclopedia of Predators*. I read to him about the evil Threggs, reminding him how we defeated their Earth invasion by playing music to them. Pluke wanted more so we studied the sinister Valloons (who pose as rainbow fairies before mincing you with tiny jewelled scissors), the Kleeenex (who look like gigantic Earth bogeys) and the Globacious Glybs (who eat several planets at one sitting).

Pluke loved it, but even he started whimpering as we read about the Wiffly Biffly. Remember them? Your ninth grandfather met one on his trip to the Bode Galaxy and returned quite mad, having lost all his heads and therefore all his minds. Wiffly Biffly look cuddly, like fluffy pink balls, but they may be the most villainous species in all the galaxies, Rok. They eat their own grandparents.

Pluke is now snoozing peacefully, but I am lying awake worrying about finding mermaids and centaurs and rescuing Pluke's puppies. So goodnight, Rok. You will be snoozing under our five moons, while I'm in my hard, flat bed again, instead of hanging upside down from an *urqflurble* chatting to you. I cannot even find any clever little flies* to talk to and I feel so alone.

Flowk

---

* Flies, I have discovered, when threatened by cold temperatures or lack of food, can temporarily shut themselves down in a process called diapause. I told you they were clever.

Dear Rok,

My friends the flies all woke up and are scampering about cheerfully with some mice. Mama discovered a 'boiler', which sends steaming H_2O through a series of tubes all round the house so it's nice and warm now.

Papa and Bert are busy rebuilding the Improver, the machine for Improving Earthlings. It will add brains and limbs and loyalty to Earthlings to make them useful slaves on Faa. I'm glad they are only planning to Improve grown-ups, so I don't have to worry about hurting my school friends. Younglings do have *some* feelings (even though they eat nice pets like 'chickens' and 'lambs' and do poo-poos actually *inside* their own houses) but I don't believe adult Earthlings have any feelings because they flatten each other with cars and wars.

Bert was trying to stop me going out of the door to school. He was *skidoodling* around the house, lights flashing, antennae whirring, burbling and bleeping excitedly. Before I knew it, he had thrown so many Earthling hats, sheep-fluff neck-winders, coats, boots, digit-wrappers and ear-flaps at me that I disappeared under a mountain of them. Pluke pulled them off me, yapping anxiously.

'What's the matter, Bert?' I asked. I couldn't help laughing. Maybe I'm developing an Earth 'sense of humour'. Bert blibbered away, sending an infostream into my data-processing head.

'Oh,' I realised. 'It's the weather report.'

Bert's lights flashed eagerly. We opened the door and of course he was right, as usual. I could hardly see the street for big white lumps of frozen H_2O floating down and making a thick freezing carpet on the ground.

'They're called snowballs,' Bert said. 'Keep warm. You don't want to catch an Earthling cold.'

'Atishoo' is a representation of the Earthling bogey eruption called a 'sneeze'. Perhaps that is why Earthlings use 'a tissue' for their exploding beaks.

The cure for the common cold is... ATISHOOO!

Farteeta says this germ causes Earthling colds. It's been trying to tell her the cure but always sneezes before it can finish.

Taking his advice, I put on more wrappings and set off for school with light hearts, quite looking forward to seeing my friends again. My wretched Earth feet skidded all over the place – Earthlings can somehow master these repulsive weather conditions with only two limbs, Rok, but I longed to unfurl my suckers or zoom above it all.

When I finally arrived at the school gates everyone was moaning that they were open. Earthlings hate learning and often shut the schools if there are a few snowballs.

Roddy flapped up to me. 'Hi Nigel, I thought you were on a spaceship,' he said.

'You have a wonderful imagination,' I replied. I'd brought the memory blaster to school so I blasted nice Roddy and nasty Colin Snell since they're the only people we didn't memory blast on our last visit. I couldn't risk them remembering my true identity, Rok.

On the way to swimming everyone seemed to like the freezing lumps. Colin Snell loved stuffing them under my neck-wrapper and in my 'welly boots'. Even Susan and Roddy threw some at me. And I thought they were my friends.

I fell over twenty-six times until, just as we approached the swimming pool, we were confronted by a white giant with fearsome black eyeballs and a pointy orange beak, like a flesh-eating *graanyark*.

'Watch out! Don't let him eat you!' I shouted, grabbing Susan and causing us both to skid into a pink-faced female carrying a woolly bundle. Unfortunately the bundle was a baby Earthling, who shrieked like a herd of *nyerds*. Fortunately the orange-beaked giant just watched while the Earthling female shouted rude words. Susan smiled at the red squealing baby, which she seemed to *like*, and apologised to the red squealing female.

'We're so sorry,' she said, 'he's from another plan—, I mean, country. He's never seen a snowman before.' Then she pulled me into the baths, doing her nice giggle.

What did she mean, 'snowman'?

My next mistake was to wear this for our swimming lesson.

I reduced my ear trumpet volume to survive the bellowing laughter.

I partly understand this Earthling habit of 'jokes', but do not understand why they find me so amusing.

Why was my costume so much funnier than everyone else's? They all looked completely ridiculous to me.

Mama chose my 'bathing cap'

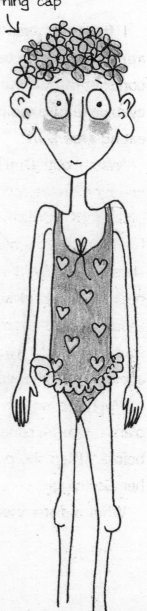

Even such a brief time away from Earthlings had made me forget how ugly they are, with their flat dull skin without fur or scales or even patterns.

* Aaron Ratchett has got fat again.

* Aaron drank Vom when we defeated the Threggs. It made him thin but it has worn off.

No wonder they usually wrap themselves up.

Anyway, to make my somehow-funny costume invisible, I threw myself into the pool. *Klong!* The cold was worse than being outside in the snow. It was such a shock that three of my tentacles shot out. I revolved them as fast as possible to stop them being seen, but it sent me up to the other end of the pool in 5.2 nanoseconds according to my third-head hypercounter. Luckily, I managed to reverse just in time so my heads didn't *phenaang* into the wall at the other end. I stuck out my compression tentacle and whizzed back the other way, creating what I think they call a 'tsunami' down here. It drenched my entire class, who squealed like a nest of *pligabooms*.

This time I was able to decelerate and Susan, who realised what was happening, ran to the edge of the pool and held up a big drying sheet (called a 'trowel') that I could wrap myself in and cover up. She brought the *Vom* too. I took a quick swig of it under the trowel and my extenders vanished.

'What on . . . er . . . Earth was that?' I said to the dripping class, whose mouths were all hanging open. 'Must have been a pressure surge in the supply pipe.'

Miss Barn was looking at me very strangely, but she just said, 'All right, class, since we're all wet, we'll get on with it. Time to practise our strokes.'

I watched for a few minutes. It was sad. Human swimming consists of very dull repetitive motions: 'crawl', 'best stroke' and 'butterfly'. Butterflies flutter by like my favourite animals here, flies, but my class was a lot clumsier getting around than them, and a lot uglier too.

Miss Barn then lined us up against the wall and flung a pile of objects into the water, which we had to rescue.

I found that one object, a big metal disc, was wedged tightly into the pool's bottom so it took me a minute or two to yank it out, keeping a sharp eyeball out for any passing mermaids. It was fun to be given a challenging task at last.

Just as I succeeded, I was hoiked out of the water by a bulgy Earthling male.

He threw me down on the pool's edge, beating my chest and pressing his mouth against mine – a revolting symbol of Earthling affection called a 'kiss'. Yeuk!

These bulgy bits are called 'muscles'. Earthlings love them.

I pushed him off and saw my class and Miss Barn with their mouths in circles and the furry lines above their eyeballs stretched high.

'Nigel!' said Miss Barn. 'You gave us a terrible fright. You stayed under for ages. Are you all right?'

Once again I'd forgotten myself. Earthlings have no gills, so they can't stay underwater for any length of time or they drown.

Everyone stared at the pool. The water was slowly draining away.

'Monster kid's pulled the plug!' Bulgy Man shouted, heaving the metal object from my hand and diving in with it. He seemed upset. 'If that ********** kid ********* again, I'll ********!' *

* This book may fall into the hands of Younglings. Please insert the words 'naughty', 'misbehaves' and 'be very cross' – Ed.

More bulgy men appeared, bells rang, and Miss Barn marched us all off to the changing rooms.

'Nigel, that was very naughty,' she said on the way back to school. 'I know the drain cover shouldn't have been left open, but you should have called for help, not tried to put it back yourself. I hope you will show more common sense next week or you won't be allowed to come on Wednesday's farm trip.'

I wanted to tell her that the five senses they have on Earth are as nothing to the 762 senses of a mature Faathing, but I couldn't risk missing the farm trip, so I apologised just like Professor McSquared told us to in his *Guide to Earth*.

'I am so very sorry, Miss Barn. I will report to the head teacher for the punishment I so richly deserve. I expect I will have to get six of the best.'

'This is no time to make silly jokes, Nigel,' she said.

Another mistake, Rok.

Teachers do not beat pupils with long sticks any more because Earthlings spend a lot of time trying not to hurt the few feelings that they have.

Professor McSquared
GUIDE TO EARTH

Volume 26 of the Exceedingly
Insignificant Planets and
Assorted Galactic
Oddities series

This, published 70 years ago, is Mama's FAVOURITE book. I tell her some of it isn't true but she won't listen.

I had to miss breaktime and write a letter of apology to the lifeguard. I took care to use my worst spelling and untidiest handwriting so it would resemble the work of an Earthling child.

Earth spellings make no sense. When Bert first taught me, I spelt 'Learner': LOLOGNYRRH.

L is 'L'.

'OLO' is 'er' as in colonel.

'GN' is 'n' as in gnat.

'YRRH' is 'er' as in myrrh.

No wonder, with spellings like these, Earthlings are such slow lolognyrrhs.

Miss Barn turned pale green (like all your great grannies) when she saw my letter. 'This is exceptional, Nigel. Wherever did you learn such long words?'

'I am uncertain what you mean, Miss Barn,' I said in my politest voice. 'The longest word I have seen in the dictionary, pneumonoultramicroscopicsilicovolcanoconiosis, is a measly forty-five letters, and the longest I have used is only eighteen letters.'

'Thank you, Nigel, please go back to your desk,' said Miss Barn, giving me a suspicious look.

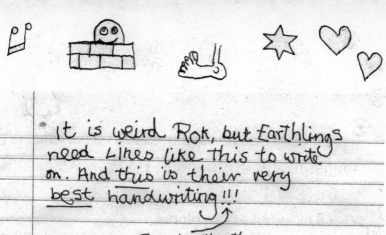

It is weird Rok, but Earthlings need lines like this to write on. And this is their very best handwriting!!!

They also like these 'exclamation marks' and use them to signify the mildest excitement. And they draw inane 'doodles' on their work.

Honestly, Rok, I have to be constantly on my guard. It's such hard work being stupid. The next longest word, hippopotomonstrosesquippedaliophobia, uses only thirty-six letters. Guess what it means? A fear of long words!

My journey home was tricky. Cars skidded scarily all over the striped road 'crossings' we're supposed to use, more snowballs flopped down from a black sky, and white giants lurked on every corner. It even felt good to be back in our little dwelling and to feel warm and dry all the way down to my blue genes, like normal.

Some of these giants have stolen 'hats' and neck wrappers after eating their prey.

Farteeta had pretended to be stupid all morning at playgroup and said it was much more fun and she's made lots of friends. She'd also rescued a goldfish. It was a lovely goldfish, but it didn't look very well.

'It doesn't seem to be working,' said Farteeta, poking it.

I'm afraid it was dead, Rok, but I didn't like to tell Farteeta, because she had taken such care of it, wrapping it up carefully in  a glove. I expect the cruel Earthlings had shortened its life with all that cold water.

I distracted Farty by showing her pictures of the ten most deadly species on Earth. They are dull compared to Faa creatures, but there is a sweet 'box jellyfish' with tentacles rather like yours. The most dangerous, the 'mosquito', is lovable like a fly, but it kills two million Earthlings a year, so it is unpopular (even though popular cars kill almost as many).

'They've all only got one head,' said Farteeta.

'Yes, that is disappointing but a few, including the charming "octopus", have multiple limbs and primitive forms of telepathy. Earthlings call it the "sixth sense" as though it's something very special. I'm hoping to get a few of these creatures

when we go on our school farm trip next week.'

Papa looped in from the garden where he has been enlarging his shed to fit the new Improver in.

'The best way to lure adult Earthlings into the Improver is to pretend it's a Health Club and Beauty Parlour,' said Mama.

'Sheds' are male Earthling nests that they make cosy with rusting tins, chisels, bits of wood, old newspapers and car engines all decorated with 'dust'. Papa's is very elegant.

And just take a look at what's INSIDE ➜

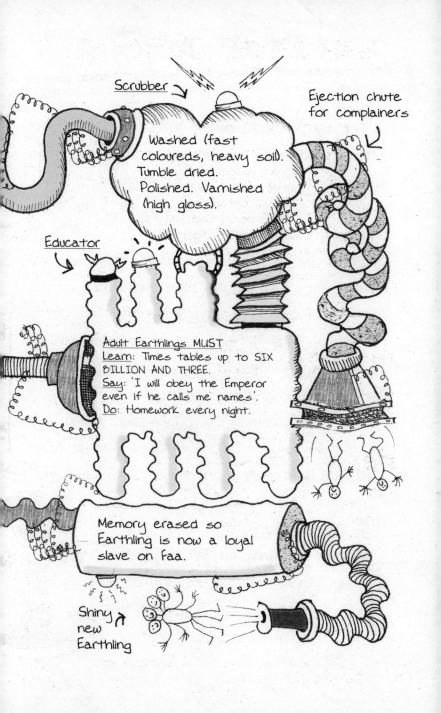

Scrubber

Ejection chute for complainers

Washed (fast coloureds, heavy soil). Tumble dried. Polished. Varnished (high gloss).

Educator

Adult Earthlings MUST
Learn: Times tables up to SIX BILLION AND THREE.
Say: 'I will obey the Emperor even if he calls me names'.
Do: Homework every night.

Memory erased so Earthling is now a loyal slave on Faa.

Shiny new Earthling

'Female Earthlings want to reduce their beak size, expand their chest bumps and get thinner all at the same time, whereas males want to move their chest wigs onto their bald heads and get big bulgy arms,' Mama went on.

'We'll give a few Earthlings big muscles and reshape their beaks, so all their friends will want a go,' said Papa. 'Then we'll flip the Improver's controls so that it really Improves Earthlings by adding four heads and limbs, turning them into useful slaves to take back to Faa.'

'You mean you're going to take away weight and add muscles to get more people to want to go in the shed, and then *really* Improve the rest?' I asked.

'Correct,' he said.

'And you're sure it will work?'

'Almost certainly, yes. We may lose a few along the way, but there are plenty more.'

'We're going to Improve the postman first,' said

Mama. 'He must really like us, because he visits every day. He brings lovely leaflets about Earthling foods and houses. I'm learning a lot from them. He is weedy and stringy, so he will want to look more "handsome".'

'Some of the creatures I am collecting will be dangerous to Earthlings, so should we keep them separately?' I asked.

'Bert is going to build this for them,' said Papa showing me a picture.

'It's called a Noah's Ark. It's the top Earthling animal transport – there are millions of references to it on their internet. We'll tow it to Faa behind our spacecraft.'

'Yes, I've seen those, but I think they are for water travel,' I said.

'How dare you question my word,' stormed Papa.

I knew better than to argue.

Poor Farteeta isn't allowed to go to playgroup any more. Bert has put his big blue plastic hoof down.

'**There is dangerousness**,' is all he will say.

'If you're going to talk, Bert, then use proper English,' said Farteeta, stamping her foot.

'It's because you're too clever, Farty,' I told her. 'If you keep doing chemistry and refusing to make pictures out of spaghetti they'll discover you're from another planet and we'll be put in the zoo, like Pluke's puppies, and we'll never get home to

Faa. Even today when you were trying to be stupid you were probably about thirty-six million times cleverer than anyone else.'

'OK,' she said, 'maybe I did make some mistakes, like when the teacher showed us a picture of Earth's sun and said it was very hot and very far away.'

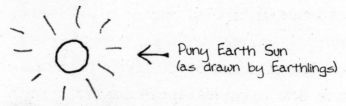

← Puny Earth Sun
(as drawn by Earthlings)

'Mmmm, and what did you say?'

'I told her it was only fifteen million degrees Celsius at its core and only ninety-three million miles away, which isn't very far at all.'

I sighed. But Mama, Papa and Bert, who don't get out of the house much, were all shocked to find out that three-year-old Earthlings don't know these simple facts.

'I'll be totally stupid on Monday, I promise. I can't stay here with Mama all day discussing *curtains*,' pleaded Farteeta.

But Bert wouldn't listen. He buzzed and fizzed while Mama carted Farteeta off to bed.

Later I asked Papa why he and Bert were being so strict.

'I might as well tell you, since you've shown how brave you are,' said Papa. 'It seems Farteeta is in danger of kidnap. By Threggs.'

Threggs. The most evil species in the Universe. I felt my neck prickle. This is called 'goose bumps'. It's like when our fur stands on end.

'But we defeated the Threggs,' I said. 'They've returned to their planet. They can't come back. And if they do, we'll defeat them again. You know they can't stand music.'

'Listen to this,' said Papa grimly.

He turned on the Interplanet, which made its usual whistling and buzzing sounds. It may be fifty gazillion times faster than Earth's internet, but it still has to trawl the entire Universe for information, so it's nothing like fast enough.

'*Booglewoogleooglenoodlepoodleapplestrudel* it,' I said.

Papa typed *Kidnap plot* into *Booglewoogleooglenoodlepoodleapplestrudel* and got 968 trillion results.

I pressed *Advanced search* and typed in, *Threggs kidnap Faathing*.

Sure enough, the horrible voice of Keith, King of Threggs, boomed through the speakers. I pressed the *Translate this page* button.

'HAR HAR HOO. HOO HOO HAR.
DEATH TO EARTH BEINGS AND INTERFERING
FAATHINGS IT GOOD WE NO MESSING HAVE OR
WE ARE MAKE MINCEMEAT DON'T BE A
SMARTASS WITH ME SUNSHINE. I SPIT IN
YOUR GENERAL DIRECTION THREGGS NEVER
DEFEATED SO UP YOUR EJECTOR SEAT
PATHETIC EARTHLINGS.
FLUFFY ALLIES IT IS ON THE MOVE.
HUMAN IMBECILES PINK ADORE. FAATHING GIRL IT
WILL BE HOSTAGE HELD UNTIL EMPIRE OF
ETERNAL SPINACH IT WILL BE OURS.
DEATH TO ALL PASSENGERS
HOOO HOO HAR!'

'It's three billion years since they invented the
translator mode and it's still rubbish,' I said.

'We know what they mean though, don't we?'
Papa said. 'The Threggs haven't been defeated,

and not only that – they've found someone else to do their dirty work.'

'But why kidnap Farteeta?'

'Small, makes an easy hostage. Also, she did the most to defeat the Threggs,' said Papa reluctantly.

'We mustn't tell her – she'll be terrified,' I said, trying to look brave and true.

'Exactly,' said Papa. 'Keep it to yourself. But these "Fluffy Allies" sound dangerous. We've got to find out what they are.'

What indeed, Rok? I've been searching my *Encyclopedia of Predators* again, looking for Fluffy Allies. Oh no! Perhaps it's the Tiny Neutrinas from the twelfth dimension, who invaded Earth around 564 million years ago and wiped out the dinosaurs. Or worse, the fluffy blue and yellow Condemnitaurs, who can disguise themselves as humans but who destroyed all the libraries and sweet shops in the fifth dimension. Or worse still, the dreaded Wiffly Biffly.

Wiffly Biffly:
rear view, legs extended.

Do not be fooled;
the Wiffly Biffly smile to lure their prey.

WIFFLY BIFFLY

Less destructive than Threggs, but more cruel and very sly.

Planet: Boffly Woffly.

Leader: Woffly Boffly.

Appearance: Charming – pink, fluffy – but don't be fooled.

Head: Singular, but large.

Body: Absent. Digestion occurs in feet. No heart is necessary, so, literally, heartless.

Legs: Bipeds. Legs extend to twice usual length.

Wings: Two. Small but exceptionally powerful.

Brain: Nineteen. Central brain sends commands to eighteen extra brains (nine in each leg).

Vision: Spectacular. Two front eyeballs have 360 degree x-ray vision, ten rear eyeballs focus across twelve galaxies.

Habits: Ravenous appetites. Cannibalism once maturity is reached, limited to devouring grandparents in order to preserve species.

Diet: Any other species (plus grandparents).

Other notes: Violently attracted to boxes, sometimes marrying them. Allergic to laughter, the colour yellow and a puddingy substance made of egg middles and cow juice.

For further details see: Horrific Habits Index, adults only section.

Didn't Keith, King of Threggs say 'Human imbeciles pink adore?' The Wiffly Biffly are fluffy *and* pink. They sounded like the only terrible creatures who could cope with being allies with the Threggs.

What with thoughts of Wiffly Biffly and all the other fluffy creatures in the Universe, and my horrid flat bed, I'm having trouble getting to sleep again. I must keep reminding myself that Earth does have nice things like chocolate and music, even if it has little else worthwhile. But alas, Rok, if we don't fulfill our Mission, you may never get to taste this wonderful taste or to hear these wonderful sounds.

Still, tomorrow is the weekend when there is no school, and we'll try out the Improver. On Sunday we'll go to the zoo to rescue Pluke's puppies and free some 'lions' and 'tigers' and 'bears'. Oh my!

Your friend in infinity,
Flowk

Dear Rok,

When I came into the living room, Mama had painted over the boring yellowy walls with black and white stripes, zigzags and random numbers so it looked like a circuit board in one of Bert's brains.

With a paintbrush in each extender she'd been able to do the whole room pretty fast by Earth standards, as well as putting out jugs of vegetables, and pictures of wildlife that Earthlings find relaxing. She had chosen adorable creatures like scorpions, tarantulas, larvae and some pretty vegetables like

Venus flytraps, so I hope the human specimens we're trying to entice into the house will like them.

Papa said Mama was nervous about the postman's visit. 'I told her to talk about the weather, which is

Earthlings' favourite topic,' he said. 'But you two had better keep out of the way while she lures him inside.'

So me and Farteeta watched from the

top of the stairs while Papa went outside to double check the Improver.

I was alarmed to see Mama didn't seem to be dressed yet. She was wearing only a frilly chest protector and matching underpants. But it was too late to warn her, because the postman was already pushing leaflets through our door, and she was swinging it open, smiling her biggest, scariest Earthling smile.

'You must be feeling colder than liquid nitrogen, you poor posting man. Come in for a nice bucket of beer,' she shrieked. (She still has no idea of how to control the volume on her Earth voice.)

At that moment, I glimpsed the horrid Colin Snell from next door passing our front gate and staring into our house with a very surprised face.

The postman looked even more surprised and started backing down our path, but Papa zoomed out to block his way. 'You are so kind to bring us all this lovely paper,' he said. 'It arrives just in time for us to wipe our bums with in the mornings. And speaking of bums, would you care for some of my wife's? She has some lovely home-baked lettuce and apricot ones in several sizes.'

'He means buns,' Farteeta whispered to me.

'I know,' I sighed. Why do parents have to be so embarrassing?

It was obvious the postman didn't want to come in. I'm getting good at reading Earthlings' facial expressions – it's not hard, because their single head can only show one thing at a time. But then Papa moved to his main point.

'How would you like to grow from this . . .' He shrunk his Earthling form so he looked like a skeleton. '. . . to THIS?' He expanded his extender muscles to three times their size so his coat and trousers split with a big ripping noise that set Pluke barking madly.

The postman's chin dropped open.

'Or from this,' said Mama, also shrinking herself, 'to THIS,' and her body suddenly bulged so that her frilly chest protector shot off with a twang and wrapped itself round the postman's head.

The postman fled into the road, bumping violently into dustbins while he pulled the chest protector off his head.

'You fool!' Papa shouted at Mama. 'What did you do that for? And for that matter, what in *Klong*'s name are you supposed to be wearing?'

Mama was covering her top part up with her tentacles (disguised as Earth arms, of course), so she was now only wearing the flowery underpants.

'Earthling males love this kind of outfit,' said Mama. 'You wait till the milkman comes.'

Just then Bert bleeped at Papa that there was a message from the Secretive Services. He rushed upstairs, shouting to me as he went, 'Tell your mother to put on more clothes and don't let anyone in till I come down.'

But once again it was too late. The milkman was at the front door, carrying the chest protector.

'Not looking for this by any chance, are you?'

'Thank you very much, I must have left it on the postman,' Mama said to him, still wrapping her tentacles around herself. 'There's something marvellous for you in our shed, as a reward for bringing us all this lovely cow juice every day to bathe in.'

The milkman now looked alarmed but Mama, not wanting to fail again, suddenly unleashed her central extender and *varoomed* the innocent fellow

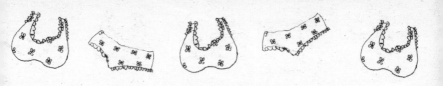

over her shoulder, into the garden and straight through the shed door.

I looped after her, but she had already pulled the *Start* lever and the Improver shimmered pink, then green and started to fizz.

Papa flew downstairs and Bert rolled after him bleeping frenziedly.

'What in *Klong*'s name are you doing?' shrieked Papa to Mama.

'The milkman loved my outfit and he has gone straight into the Improver. We have our first victim.'

'Idiot! The postman is a weedy, stringy person and the milkman is a small, fat puff. You know the Improver has to be adjusted for size and weight.'

'I thought you'd be pleased,' said Mama.

Bert and Papa frantically pulled levers and pressed buttons on the whirring, buzzing Improver.

'TERMINATE SYSTEMS AND ACTIVATE EXIT,' droned Bert.

Seconds later the milkman shot out of the ejector chute.

He looked lovely. The Improver had added heads and limbs, even if they were all in the wrong place. One head grew out of his left leg, one grew out of his chest. His original head had shrunk to the size of an eyeball, whereas another head, four times the size of his normal one, had grown out of his left foot. He had fourteen limbs sticking out in various directions.

All four of his heads burst into tears.

Bert went mental. 'REVERSE PROCEDURE.'

'Oh, stop being such a fusspot,' said Papa. 'We've made a little mistake, that's all. The controls must have slipped into Slave function instead of Muscle-building mode. Never mind, there are plenty more Earthlings. We can just put him in the bin.'

'Earthcode: banned waste-disposal items – inflammable liquids, wet batteries, dog-droppings, blood products, Earthlings alive or dead,' Bert bleeped. 'Attention also to Earthlaw regulations re: common assault, grievous bodily harm, murder...'

'All right, all right,' Papa said to Bert. 'But Earthlings kill each other all the time, so I don't see why anyone should miss him.'

'Soldiers and automobiles licensed to kill,' announced Bert. 'Not we. Must rescue Improver subject. Reverse procedure.'

Papa reluctantly bundled the weepy milkman back into the Improver and pressed *Reverse*, despite Bert bleeping loudly.

We all held our breath.

But what came out of the Improver was not the same milkman as when he went in. It was a baby milkman, wailing like the fat, red baby at the swimming pool.

'You're hopeless,' said Farteeta. 'You've reversed him through time. He's gone back to being how he

was years ago.' She ran to pick up the baby milkman who howled even louder, while Farteeta gave Papa instructions on how to work the Improver.

'I knew all that,' grumbled Bert, 'but he wouldn't listen to me.'

The baby squawled louder still and Mr Snell from next door poked his head over the fence.

'What is that row? And I said you needed planning permission for that eyesore of a shed. Now it's twice the size. I'm calling the council.'

Luckily, Bert was inside the shed with the Improver and so was not visible to Mr Snell. But Mama's unfortunate clothing arrangements were very visible indeed. Mr Snell turned pink and bobbed down out of sight muttering, 'You'll catch your death, more snow on the way.'

The baby milkman was now yelling at 110 decibels.

'Put him back in, we must stop this awful racket,' said Mama.

'Improver not fixed in nanoseconds, needs adjustment,' bleeped Bert, irritated. 'Earthling infants soothed by lullaby song function or nutrition from parent's chest bumps, bottom cleansing and tentacle wrapping.'

'They like cow juice,' said Farteeta, offering the baby one of the milkman's bottles. But it only yelled louder.

'Quick,' said Mama to me. 'Get some ice cream from the shop on the corner to shut it up. That's made from cow juice and all Earthling children love it.'

I zoomed off. I had never been inside a shop, but it was crammed with all the strange things Earthlings need (masses of stuff for looking after their small amounts of hairstyle and polishing their chewing blades, underarm painters to reduce their smell, elastic bands, paperclips). I asked a lady (it was definitely a lady because it was wearing a skirty thing) for ice cream.

'In the freezer, sweetheart.'

I thought that was a rather inappropriate comment. I followed where she pointed and – HORRORS – I had to pass a stack of those rolled up papers that Earthlings use to wipe their poo-poos. Bravely I did it, repressing all my olfactory systems, snatched the ice cream from the freezer and hurried out. I couldn't bear to pass those piles of toilet papers again.

As I left I heard the female yelling, 'Come back, you naughty boy. You haven't paid!'*

I zoomed back to the yelling milkman, tore open the package and thrust a bar into its mouth. It spat it out with alarming velocity.

'That's not ice cream,' said Farteeta, looking at the packet. 'It's fishfingers.'

Can you believe that Earthlings actually cut the fingers off little fishes and freeze them?

Luckily Bert and Farteeta had by now fixed the Improver, this time putting it in Muscle-building mode, so we fed the squawling miniature milkman back in and held our breaths again.

After much loud grunting and juddering, the Improver shimmered yellow and green, hissed and spat out the milkman.

* She actually said something much ruder than this, which I am not allowed to repeat.

He was his grown-up self again, only taller and with bulgy arms like the swimming pool lifeguard. And he had grown a hairstyle.

'I got a six pack now,' he said, smiling at his chest. Then he ran his fingers through his new hairstyle. 'You could make a fortune with this.'

'My wife will give you leaflets so you can tell all your friends,' Mama said, gesturing at Papa who was just emerging from the shed.

'Your wife?' said the milkman, staring at Papa.

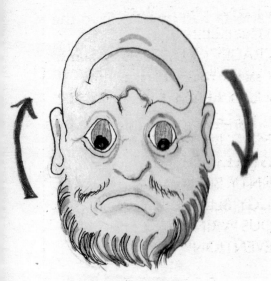

The milkman didn't look too happy when he went into the improver. But TURN HIM UPSIDE DOWN to see how happy he is with his new hairstyle.

'She means husband, of course, she's a little the worse for wear,' said Papa. 'And worse, she's wearing far too little,' he added, giving the milkman a bundle of leaflets and waving lots of paper 'money' at him. 'If you distribute these to all the houses you visit, I will give you thousands of pounds.'

FREE HEALTH CLUB AND
BEAUTY PARLOUR
ENORMOUS OPENING

FRYDAY X O'CLOCK ANTE MERIDIAN
FEMALES VERY WELCOME!!!!!
EDIBLES AND BEVERAGES (Whisky, lettuce bums, cow juice soda, fried salads, roasted loaves, etc.)
BUILD NICE BIG BULGY ARMS AND BOTTOMS!
FURRY HEADS FOR MALES!
BIG, BOUNCY CHEST BUMPS FOR LADIES!!!!!
EXPLODING HAIRSTYLES FOR ALL!
SHRINK LONG POINTY BEAKS!
LOSE WOBBLY BAGGY BLUBBER!
IRON YOUR HIDEOUS WRINKLES!
FACE FALLING PREVENTION!

'No, no, use this version I made,' said Farteeta, thrusting an even bigger bunch of leaflets at the dazed milkman, who tottered off, whistling.

<u>GRAND OPENING</u>
FREE HEALTH CLUB AND BEAUTY SALON

FRIDAY 10am
Snacks and drinks served.

ALL WELCOME!!

BUILD MUSCLES
BODY RESHAPING AND TONING
EXPERT HAIRSTYLING
LOSE WEIGHT
SMOOTH WRINKLES
FACE LIFTS
Enjoy our gorgeous, relaxing atmosphere.

Tomorrow we're off to the zoo to rescue Pluke's puppies and catch creatures. Susan is coming too.

Your friend in infinity,

Flowk

Hey Rok,

Susan's mum is a bus driver and she offered to drive Susan and me to the zoo in her big red bus. Papa kicked up a fuss as usual.

'I know Earthlings let their females drive, but I'm not having you being driven by one.'

'But dopey Flyzoop drives us across a squillion galaxies,' I said.

Papa relented, and then gave me a mobile phone. 'These are pathetic devices Earthlings use because they have no telepathy,' he said. 'But it means you can ring the emergency services if you're in trouble.'

Farteeta handed me a parcel as we left. 'Could be useful,' she said.

Inside the bus was attractive. The floor was blueish grey and speckly (just like your cousins), and the seats were squiggly orange, brown and blue (like the Emperor's favourite wife). It is a jerky form of transportation, Rok. Many elderly Earthlings seemed in fear of their safety as they mounted and dismounted at the various stopping places. And it is full of confusing instructions, like *Emergency Exit* and *Priority Seats*. There is even one telling you to *Break Glass*.

Susan told me this symbol means 'No smoking'.

I know that we sizzle and smoke when all four of our heads are angry, but I have not seen anyone here do it yet, so I asked Susan when Earthlings smoke. She said it has nothing to do with their feelings, but to do with little paper tubes full of toxins they put in their mouths and set light to – for fun!

Looking out of the windows made me think Earthlings must get very bored with their own thoughts because they put up big pictures to look at everywhere they go. They even have them on the inside walls of the bus.

You'd think these must be pictures of very exciting things to combat Earthling boredom, but they show Earthlings doing absolutely nothing interesting at all – just smiling their horrible smiles while sitting in cars, standing in kitchens, holding infants, lying on sand, or combing their hairstyles. Mama was right about chest protectors and underpants though – lots of female Earthlings in the pictures are dressed like that.

Susan told me these pictures are 'advertisements'. They show nicer cars, kitchens, hairstyles, sand-lying places, or infants than most Earthlings have, and say that if Earthlings spent lots of money, they could get these nicer ones and it would make them happier.

Words like *NEW, BEST, FREE, HEALTHY* appear a lot, for things that aren't new, are exactly the same as other things, cost money and are bad for you.

But soon our journey became more interesting. The streets grew frighteningly crowded and the dwellings were stretched, as if someone had piled many measly houses like ours on top of each other. Red, green and orange lights constantly flashed on the streets, apparently because Earthlings can't foresee contact with approaching objects and need guiding like blind *plurnwooms*, at every obstacle.

I did spot several wonderful new creatures on wheels, though. They resembled Earthlings in some respects, but were clearly invincible, weaving among all the random scary cars, rather like our *nardoons*.

'What are they called?' I asked Susan.

'Cyclists,' she said.

'Are they a dominant species? Or a pet?'

Susan looked at me as if I was from outer space. (Ho ho. You see, I *am* beginning to understand jokes.)

'They're people, silly,' she said. 'Sorry, but I keep forgetting how little you know.'

I thought this was unfair coming from someone who hasn't even experienced the fourth dimension.

'So why don't you grow some wheels like them? That is much better than your sluggish walking.'

'It's a bicycle,' she said. 'It's a person on a bicycle. The fast ones are motorbikes. They're not different creatures.'

I watched the cyclists closely and soon I could tell that they *were* actually Earthlings riding on machines.

'Susan! Nigel! Here we are,' Susan's mum called. 'I'll be back this way in two hours, so mind you're waiting at the stop,' she said, and we tumbled off.

Luckily Mama had given me some of the money she'd made on our printer, so I was able to pay for our tickets.

Well, Rok, apart from music, the zoo was the best thing I've encountered on Earth yet. There is a great diversity among Earth creatures and they are most intelligent. But many of them are enormous. I'd expected them to be the size of poodles.

The giraffe, for example, is a noble beast some five metres high, elegantly evolved so it can nibble tall vegetables, and it's covered in pleasant dapples. It is comforting to see something as big as I usually am, but it would not have fitted into Susan's mum's bus.

I was wondering if I could take at least one monkey home, since they are the size of a human child. Earthlings evolved from monkeys only a couple of million years ago, which shows how evolution can backfire, since monkeys have been sensible enough to retain their fur and eat vegetables and have no need of clothes or money.

On Faa, evolution always improves species. Yet human ancestors are infinitely more attractive than humans are.

The animals were very excited to see me. They have far more acute sensory systems than humans and could sense my alien presence. My transspecies translation lobe also had no problem with the languages of these creatures, so it was easy to converse with them. I was sad to discover that they were not very happy to be in their enclosures, but wanted, they said, to run free. I have a mind to release them all, but must be content with only rescuing a few for now.

The lions, kings of the beasts, were among the first to make contact, hurling themselves towards me in greeting. I feel sure they recognised a kindred spirit, because the Emperor says we Faathings are kings of the Universe.

'They seem to like you,' Susan whispered, staring at them with very round eyes. I could hardly hear her for all the expressions of greeting transmitted from the lions, even though to Susan they

seemed only to be baring their teeth, yawning, or
making the occasional growl.

Lions are born free
but everywhere they
are in cages.

'You can have no
idea, mate,' the first lion was saying to me, 'what a
pleasure it is to finally meet somebody you can have
a sensible conversation with. 'Scuse me for asking,

but what's a class act like you doing hanging out with a wildebeest like her?'

'She's a friend of mine,' I told him. 'Not all humans are that bad.'

The lion considered this. 'Our keeper's not too bad, as it goes. If only he wouldn't keep calling me Simba when my name's Darren.'

The lions recommended a chat with the elephants, who they said were the only other animals worth talking to in the zoo. Susan hadn't been able to hear any of this, of course, and I'm not sure she believed it when I told her, but we went off to talk to them anyway.

'Have you come far?' asked the largest one.

'We've come from Faa, yes,' I said to him.

'Quite so, quite so. Excuse me, would you mind if I take a shower?'

The elephant put his long tubular beak into a big tub of water, sucked a lot in, then sprayed it all over himself. Susan clapped. But how will I capture this magnificent beast? And even if I do, how will I transport it to our ridiculously small house, and where will I keep it?

I must confess, Rok, I have not thought my Mission through very carefully.

'Time to rescue Pluke's puppies now,' Susan whispered. I had been so worried about the surprising size of all the animals that I had forgotten all about the puppies. We followed the signs:

PUPPIES FROM OUTER SPACE?

OR BRAND NEW SPECIES?

OUR SCIENTISTS

ARE INVESTIGATING.

VIEWING TIME

2 P.M. – 4 P.M.

The queue to see Pluke's puppies stretched almost round the whole zoo. Another bizarre Earthling habit is to stand in queues for almost anything, whereas we would just go off and find something else to do.

We sat on a bench to work out a plan.

'Hey, Farteeta gave you a package as we left, saying it could be useful, didn't she? What was in it?' asked Susan.

We opened Farteeta's parcel. It was a big, dark Earthling coat and a hat with the words *Zoo Keeper* written on it in gold letters.

'What's the point of that?' I shrugged.

'Farty's *so* clever,' said Susan, picking up the coat. 'But we're too small. Can you extend your suckers to look like a grown up?'

'Not for long,' I replied. 'My whole disguise would dissolve if I let my suckers out for more than a few minutes.'

'Well then, you sit on my shoulders and we'll

90

drape the coat over us both and you can put on the cap. Then we'll be able to walk past everyone.'

So that is what we did.

When people saw the words *Zoo Keeper* on my cap they just moved aside and we wobbled to the front of the queue.

Our luck was in, Rok. It was nearly four o' clock and the puppies had been moved from their nice enclosure full of toys and treats to a small cage ready to be taken off for their tea. They recognised me immediately, running up to the front of the cage, werfing and dribbling.

I adjusted my vocal apparatus to a deeper setting (human males have to 'break' their voices when they become men), said 'Feeding time', picked up the little cage and strode out. Or rather, Susan strode out, with me clinging on for dear life. She was peeping through the coat buttons but even so we kept bumping into people on the way.

'That's not fair, we haven't seen the
puppies properly,'
wailed a small child,
poking his mama in
the legs with an ice
cream. Once this
child had started,
all the others
began jumping
up and down.
Several of them
ran after me and
Susan, pulling at
our coat and
causing us to
weave about
like an
urqflurble in a
strong wind.

'Bring back the puppies, bring back the puppies,' they chanted.

'WHOAAA,' shouted Susan from under the coat, as the children pulled it as hard as they could. Earthlings have very poor balance. I knew we were about to fall over and our rescue would be ruined. I quickly stuck a gripper out to its full length, grabbed a branch, and shot upwards out of the top of the coat and into a tree with the puppies, so fast nobody saw me. Susan was staggering around in circles, a frightened coat on legs. The children all squealed.

'Man lost head!' shouted one. Somebody's mama screamed, sighed and fell down. Earthlings can go to sleep at strange times, Rok. A few children were clapping their hands, others were crying. Susan got her eye to a buttonhole and ran, keeping the coat pulled over her head, and I followed through the trees, swinging from my gripper.

'Monkey stolen puppies!' yelled the first child to

look up and see me. Alarm noises were now going off in the zoo, and real zoo keepers were running towards the crowd. But we got to some bushes round the back of the toilets just ahead of them all, popped a puppy into each pocket of the big coat, and strolled, chatting, out of the toilet area – Susan with the coat now slung over her shoulder – just as everybody else was running into it.

'Have you seen a headless running coat and a monkey with two-headed puppies?' a zoo keeper asked us as we passed.

'As a matter of fact we have, sir. They went that way,' I said and pointed in the opposite direction to the exit.

Everyone headed off that way, and Susan and I wandered out of the zoo. My zoo keeper's uniform had looked nothing like the real zoo keepers'*, but

* I discovered later that Farteeta found the hat in the 'toy box' and the coat in Papa's Earthling disguises.

luckily Earthlings obey people in uniforms. If someone dressed as a doctor asks them to remove all their clothes, they will. If someone puts on a white coat and calls themselves a dentist, Earthlings will let them remove all their chewing blades. I've seen in books that even Earthling burglars have uniforms of striped tops and masks, which must make it very easy to catch them.

We stood at the bus stop listening to the sirens and loudspeakers and two minutes later Susan's

mum arrived in her bus and dropped me back near our house.

Pluke was ecstatic to see his children again. The Snells mustn't know they're here, so we have made a nest for them in my bedroom.

Papa said we had enough to worry about without ten extra mouths to feed. 'They could be the Fluffy Allies that the Threggs were talking about.'

'Papa, they are Pluke's very own puppies,' I reminded him. 'And I think the Fluffy Allies may be the Wiffly Biffly.'

'Hah!' he said, glancing briefly at the *Encyclopedia of Predators*. 'You may have proved yourself brave and true, but we are looking for something far more sinister than a furry ball. Something with claws and vileness, fanged and smileless, cunning yet —'

'Yes, yes,' I said. Papa can get carried away when he starts making a heroic speech. 'But we mustn't underestimate the Wiffly Biffly. There are terrible

stories all over the Universe about their ruthlessness. And Keith, King of Threggs, said something about pink, didn't he? The Wiffly Biffly are pink, as well as fluffy. I know, because Rok's ninth grandfather told us —'

'A garbled translation from a Thregg and evidence from a Faathing who lost all of his minds will hardly convince me, Flowkwee,' Papa said.

I couldn't persuade Papa about the Wiffly Biffly so I went to see Bert in his den and ask if he believed it. Bert has the biggest room in the house because he fills it up with loads of wires, pliers, levers, cleavers, wheels, steel, catapults, dogapults, funnels, tunnels, triggers, diggers and all kinds of other contraptions that often turn out to be amazing inventions. It was more crowded with random stuff than usual, a lot of it piled up in a heap of cables and twisted tubes in the corner, which I fell over on the way in.

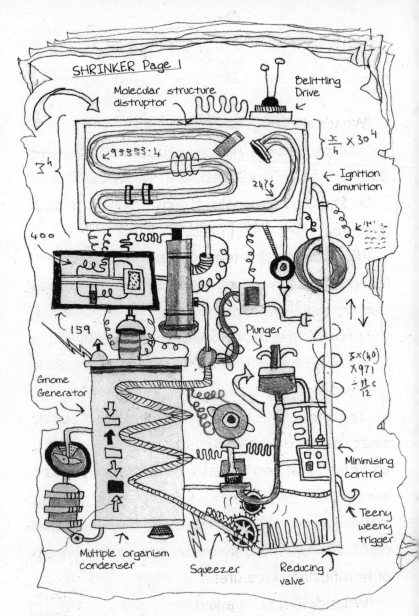

There are a <u>hundred</u> pages of Bert's
SHRINKER diagram . . .

'What's all this?' I asked him.

'Shrinker,' Bert snapped. 'Intended to use against Fluffy Allies. But no good.'

'A Shrinker? To make things smaller?' I said. 'Bert, that's just what I need.'

'No good,' repeated Bert sounding annoyed. 'Supposed to disrupt molecular structures and condense multiple organisms – but data corrupted, hacked off with it, no good.'

'We might need it,' I told him. 'The Wiffly Biffly are coming.'

'Incorrect. Fourteen million fluffy species in nearby galaxies. Wiffly Biffly low on list of suspects. If enemy is Wiffly Biffly, alternative deterrent needed,' said Bert, hitting buttons on his module megadrive, and scrolling down lists of horrific fluffy creatures.

'What deterrent?' I asked.

'Saturated fat, protein, calcium...'

'Custard,' I said, flicking through my memory bank of Earthling foods. 'Susan and Roddy have it every day for school dinner.'

Bert said nothing, but bleeped to himself quietly for a while. He hates admitting I know something he doesn't.

'It's an Earthling pudding, Bert,' I insisted. 'A cooked mixture of cow juice and egg middles. What does it do to the Wiffly Biffly?'

'Fluff erasure, acute temperature loss, rapid-onset identity crisis.'

'Their hair falls out, then they get cold and embarrassed?'

'Correct. And what attracts them is blatkerzoopyfloom,' Bert said, but I could see only about a tenth of his circuits were engaged with the issue.

'That's cellulose, lignin and various carbohydrate polymers down here,' I said, computing quickly. 'In a word, cardboard.'

'**Blatkerzoopyfloom**,' Bert corrected, always a stickler for the right terminology. '**Wiffly Biffly do anything for it.**'

'That's right, Bert. The encyclopedia said they like boxes, so I suppose that means cardboard, and they are allergic to yellow. Custard is yellow.'

'**Earth butter yellow! Earth jumpers yellow! Earth flowers yellow! Dim little puny Earth sun yellow! No reason for Wiffly Biffly to come here. Plenty of planets with no yellow!**'

Well, if I couldn't persuade Bert that the Wiffly Biffly were our enemy, I could at least pursue my other plan.

'Dear Bertle Wertle,' I coaxed, 'can I ask you for a favour? Will you have another go at making

your Shrinker work? We really need it to capture the animal samples for the Mission. Many of the zoo animals are very big.'

Bert went quiet and just hummed. I think he's feeling the pressure of so much depending on him.

'OK Bert,' I said. 'I'll leave you to it. But can I borrow your Shrinker bits for a while?'

Bert didn't seem to care one way or the other. I hope he's not on the verge of a circuit breakdown. I dragged the pile of Shrinker parts out of the door and closed it quietly.

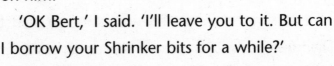

How am I going to make sense of his diagrams, Rok? Still, double maths tomorrow. Hooray.

Flowk

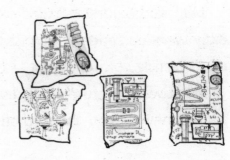

Dear Rok,

Mama is very excited because her new 'vacuum cleaner' has arrived.

'It sucks up all the dust even better than a slave,' she warbled at breakfast. 'Come and help me vacuum the snow.'

'No,' said Farteeta. 'I am fed up of ironing the carpets and straightening up the kettles. I hate you all. Especially you,' she said, kicking me.

'What was that for?' I asked.

'You never even thanked me for helping you

rescue Pluke's puppies,' she hissed.

'I'm sorry, Farty. I know you're grumpy staying home all day while I go to school. But listen, there is something you can help me with.' And I showed her Bert's Shrinker parts and diagrams.

She cheered up then as she loves a challenge.

At the school gates everyone was talking about the puppies being stolen from the zoo.

Colin Snell was waving the paper around.

'They're OUR puppies, we want them back,' he was shouting.

'I thought your dad sold them to some scientists,' said Susan.

Colin spotted me and changed the subject. 'Oh, hello Nigel. Why was your mum talking to the postman in her underwear?'

I could see he meant something nasty because Orville Muffin nudged Aaron Ratchett and they both smirked.

Double maths was disappointing, Rok. I thought it would mean doubly difficult, but it just meant two lessons in a row.

We were doing a 'maths olympics' which is Miss Barn's way of trying to make maths fun. Sadly her worksheets were far too simple to resemble fun to me, Rok.

$$2 + 8 - 1 = ? \quad 3 \times 4 = ?$$

As you can see, Rok, these sums are horrifically simple.

$$3\sqrt{360000} \times 4^{12}\ \vdash\ \times\ \frac{300{,}000^2}{46900}$$

She promised a smiley face sticker to the first to finish, but I have learnt not to be best at everything, so instead I amused myself thinking about some of Earth's most difficult maths problems. Bert told me about the Riemann hypothesis, which remains unsolved on Earth, even though it is clearly the same as Toonfloot's theorem, which Faa mathematicians proved in the fourth Quadratic period.

I decided to solve it before the end of the lesson.

'What's that doodling? Where's your worksheet, Nigel?' said Miss Barn, peering at my calculations.

'It's about the patterns of prime numbers, Miss Barn,' I said. 'Computers have shown the first ten trillion zeroes in this sequence fall in a geometrical pattern, but you've yet to find out how it mirrors energy patterns in atoms.'

'What on Earth are you talking about, Nigel?'

'Sorry, Miss Barn, I don't know what came over

$$\zeta(s) = \sum_{n=1}^{\infty} \frac{1}{n^s} = \frac{1}{1^s} + \frac{1}{2^s} + \frac{1}{3^s} + \ldots$$

$$\left(1 - \frac{2}{2^s}\right)\zeta(s) = \sum_{n=1}^{\infty} \frac{(-1)^{n+1}}{n^s} = \frac{1}{1^s}$$

$$-\frac{1}{2^s} - \frac{1}{3^s} - \frac{1}{4^s} - \frac{1}{5^s} - \frac{1}{6^s}$$

$$\zeta(s) = 2^s \, \pi^{s-1} \sin\left(\frac{\pi s}{2}\right)$$

$$\Gamma(1-s) \, \zeta(1-s)$$

$$Li(x) = \int_0^x \frac{dt}{\log(t)}$$

$$|\pi(x) - Li(x)| < \frac{1}{8\pi} \sqrt{x} \, \log(x)$$

$$fo$$

me. I found the worksheets you gave us rather difficult,' I said quickly. 'Maths is not my best subject.'

Miss Barn looked relieved. 'Perhaps you had better go into the Wolves group, dear,' she said. So I sat with Annie Spratt and Aaron Ratchett, making shapes out of paper. Annie Spratt was crying as usual.

To cheer her up, I made a six-dimensional cube, a few flying ozoids and a couple of octagonal pyramids.

They looked like the ones on Planet Qwertyuiop.*
Everyone crowded round the Wolves' table.

'Wicked,' said Orville Muffin. I know this means good, so I was pleased.

'Amazing origami,' said Jatinder. 'Show me how to do it.' My hypermood evaluator told me the general level of amazement was higher than it should be, so I crumpled my designs before Miss Barn could start saying I was a genius.

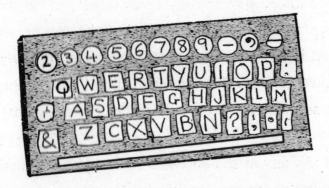

* The first Earth keyboard was invented by a visitor from planet QWERTYUIOP, which explains the weird top line of letters that Earthlings still use today.

Back home there was the usual mayhem about the Improver and the identity of the Fluffy Allies.

Farteeta was struggling with Bert's Shrinker parts. 'It's harder than it looks,' was all she would say when I asked her how she was getting on.

Mama is happy because the milkman came for more leaflets, but she's worried that she has done something wrong.

'I showed him my lovely pictures and he said they were very modern. That's good, isn't it?' she asked nervously. 'It's just that he asked if his wife could stay in the kitchen when she comes, as she's got an Earth disease called arachnophobia. That's not catching is it?'

'It's a fear of spiders,' said Farteeta. 'Maybe you should just leave up the vegetable pictures.'

Me and Farteeta reorganised the pictures so we now only have the broccoli and toadstools which

I think does look nicer.

Meanwhile I have to wear my beak muffler even in bed, since the puppies are doing poo-poos all over my room. A comforting thing is that my friends the flies seem to like my room best now, so there are hundreds of them in here to keep me company.

Trying hard to look on the bright side,
Flowk

↖ Have discovered this vegetable eats my little fly friends, so have removed it from the wall.

MISSION EARTH TWO:
DAY SIX - TUESDAY

Hey Rok,

We had indoor PE instead of football today, because fresh snowballs fell during the night.

Miss Barn had arranged an 'obstacle course' – a simple climbing unit consisting of trestles, horizontal poles, benches, hoops and two ladders, very like the tentacle-exercising equipment we use with new-born babies on Faa. Unfortunately I found myself first in line, whereas I should have waited to see what everyone else did.

Earthlings take ages to learn even very simple things, like walking.

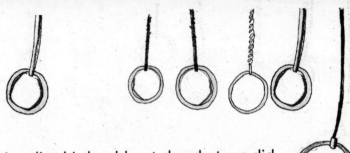

I realised I should not do what we did as babies, flexing our suckers and looping through the hoops before skimming horizontally through each ladder rung and accelerating to near light speed to complete the course. You were very good at that, Rok.

So I kept it simple. I walked slowly along the bench on my grippers, dived through the hoop feet first and spun up the ladder on my head (taking care to look clumsy and miss a few rungs). Then I calculated the angle between the ladder and the trestles so as to bounce off each pole in turn, missed out the second hoop so as to look foolish, and executed a triple somersault onto the mat. My timing was approximately 4.5 seconds, or a squillion times longer than I would normally take.

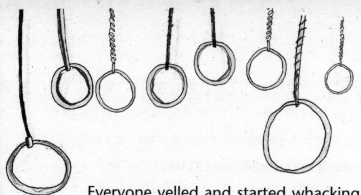

Everyone yelled and started whacking me so I knew I'd been too good again.

'His family are in a circus,' Susan helpfully explained to Miss Barn.

'How lovely,' said Miss Barn. 'Perhaps you could demonstrate some juggling at the school fair, Nigel?'

Everyone else lumbered round the course. Roddy couldn't even get through the first hoop and started flapping his arms.

'You're such a weirdo,' hissed Colin Snell, which made Roddy flap even more. Then he pulled his sweatshirt over his head and went to sit in the corner of the hall.

When Colin Snell's turn came I flipped out my extension sucker at lightning speed and moved the bench so that he fell flat on the mat and everybody laughed at him, which he hates.

'It moved!' he protested to Miss Barn.

'Of course it didn't, Colin,' she said. 'But nobody minds if you don't know how to do it.'

At lunch I sat with Roddy, who was looking sad.

'Nobody likes me because I'm weird,' he said.

'I like you. I'm weird too,' I told him.

He flapped his arms and smiled and my hearts expanded.

After lunch it was still too cold to play outside so we watched an ancient 'film'. It was just in black and white and had no speech but strange, clangy music. All the Earthlings moved about very fast and kept falling off ladders or down holes and slipped over on banana skins that untidy people seemed to keep leaving on the floor. At the end they all threw puddings at each other. I thought it must be a film to teach us how to be tidy and careful, but everyone

This is a 'banana skin' a yellow vegetable that humans like to slip on.

← custard
pie

kept laughing at it, including Miss Barn, so it must be another of those incomprehensible Earthling jokes.

The one sense that Earthlings seem to have that we don't is what they call a sense of humour. They seem to like to escape difficult things by laughing.

Miss Barn said the puddings they were throwing were 'custard pies', which made me think of the Wiffly Biffly, and how this noxious yellow *gloo-poglious* substance called custard frightened them, when Earthlings find it funny.

At home time, Miss Barn reminded us about our farm trip. 'Bring warm clothes,' she said.

I hope the farm animals will be smaller than the zoo animals, Rok. In some of the school library books cows are drawn the same size as hamsters, but in others they look as large as elephants.

'I've got something to show you,' said Farteeta when I got home. She beckoned me upstairs.

Farty's amazing SHRINKER.
How does she do it?

'Allow me to introduce you to Farty's fabulous condensing compressing constricting dwindling minimising reducing Shrinker.'

I recognised some of the wires and tubes I'd rescued from Bert's den, but they were now neatly assembled together into a small and gleaming machine. It's another reminder, Rok, that I shouldn't underestimate Farteeta, even though she's a baby compared to me, and a female as well.

'Look,' she said, pointing the Shrinker at her

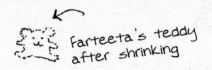

Farteeta's teddy after shrinking

biggest teddy. (This is a pretend pet that Earthling children share their beds with.)

There was a puff of smoke and the teddy wobbled, shivered, went blurry at the edges and dissolved to a tiny teddy-shaped drop. It was only just visible.

'*Arakatoon!* But what about living things?'

'Here's a mouse I did earlier,' said Farty, proudly brandishing a small box. She opened it a fraction and a tiny creature jumped out and fled under the bed. 'I've done six mice and twenty flies. I've been doing it all day. The flies got too small to see but the mice are just visible. It has a reverse mode too, in case you shrink something by mistake, and the effect only lasts for two or three days anyway so your fly friends will be their normal size again soon.'

'Don't show it to Bert – he'll say it's no good because he didn't do it,' I said.

'I did,' replied Farteeta, grinning. 'And he did. But it's smaller and simpler than what he was trying to build. He wanted to shrink the Threggs and their horrible allies. This one won't work on them, or even on humans, but it'll do to get the animals out of the zoo.'

'Farty, it's brilliant!' I said, hugging her.

'You haven't done that for a long time,' she said.

'Well, it's because you're so ugly as a human. I miss your pretty violet scales,' I replied.

I am going back to the zoo at three a.m. in the morning, with the Shrinker. I've texted* Susan and she's coming too. She is really excited about freeing the animals from captivity, which is weird as she is perfectly happy to eat them and wear them.

I'll update you later,
Flowk

* 'Texting' is the Earthling word for sending messages on mobile phones.

MISSION EARTH TWO:
DAY SEVEN - WEDNESDAY

Hi Rok,

Papa and Bert were still up at two a.m., fuming and raving in Bert's den.

'They're getting closer,' I could hear Papa saying. 'The Threggs are on standby in the Andromeda Galaxy. But the Fluffy Allies have blocked our signal so we've lost contact with the Secretive Services. They could be here by the weekend and we still don't know what they are.'

I crept back to my bedroom since I didn't want to risk Papa telling me not to go out alone at night.

He's becoming more and more fearful, like Earthling parents who don't even let their children walk to school by themselves. Susan had told me there were no Earthlings about at three a.m., so I reckoned it was safe to fly to the zoo.

I slipped out of the window and landed 0.1 nanoseconds later on Susan's windowsill. She jumped on my shoulders, carrying a bag full of little boxes for our animal samples, and we sprang into the air. I quickly had to divert vertically, with Susan's arms tightening around my neck, when a brown flying creature veered into our path, hooting loudly.

'What was that?' I shouted to Susan.

'An owl,' she said excitedly. 'Wasn't it lovely?'

'No, it was very rude,' I told her. 'I won't repeat what it said about my flying.'

We flew on towards the zoo. I was careful not to go higher than 3000 Earth metres, above which

TOO WIT
TOO WOO
*

* <u>Translation</u>: 'Watch where you're going you ~~████████████~~ (sorry, the publisher has censored this as unsuitable for younglings).

Susan's breathing apparatus doesn't work. We passed a church belfry full of bats, which swarmed out at us, gibbering excitedly in high-pitched voices about their plans to join with ants and dolphins in a bid for World Domination. Can't come too soon for me. They will run planet Earth much better than humans. Bats are spectacular pilots, Rok. Flyzoop could take lessons from the way they seem about to hit you then turn away at the last nanosecond.

'They must have amazing vision,' said Susan.

'They can't see at all,' I told her. 'They just bounce squeaks off things.' I shrank two (so they wouldn't be lonely), and put them in a box. Then I shot upwards, seeing a plane, and for a while we flew alongside. The pilot saw us, and Susan gave him a wave. He waved back with both arms, his mouth wide open, then in his confusion must have done something wrong to the controls, because the plane tipped sideways and started falling. All the Earthlings inside opened their mouths very wide too. I flew under the dipping wing, calculated its flight path and velocity, and corrected it. The Earthlings all cheered.

'They think they've seen Superman,' Susan said in my ear.

What did she mean?

We could have played all night, gliding on the winds, turning somersaults that made Susan squeal at first and then giggle, soaring upwards across the

silver Earth moon, hovering between Earthlings' feeble creations and the vast roof of the glittering stars they know almost nothing about.

It felt glorious to loop and zoom again, but finally, I remembered our Mission. I think zooming with such a happy Susan must have affected my judgement, Rok (am I being infected with Earth feelings?) because when I homed in on the zoo and dived towards the target, we somehow ended up at the bottom of the penguins' pool.

I was so excited to see if the Shrinker would work on anything bigger than a bat that I zapped two of them, but not before I'd dried poor freezing Susan with my posterior heat extender.

'Weeny penguins,' hissed Susan. 'Oh, they are gorgeous!'

Susan dropped her sweetie in excitement at the little penguins.

Using my laser eye and cutting tentacle we disabled the feeble security, melted glass, bent bars and severed wires to reach the animals. The Shrinker was miraculous, reducing elephants to the size of hamsters and tigers to the size of mice. As well as these we collected zebras, pandas, chimpanzees, meerkats, rhinos, hippos, wolves, giraffes, alligators and more.

Unfortunately one of the alligators was eaten by a passing squirrel before we had time to catch it.

I was excited to find several cages of gorgon hairstyle clippings. Surely gorgons must live nearby.

'Serves it right,' said Susan. 'Alligators have no feelings.'

I wasn't sure about shrinking the lions, because I'd made friends with Darren, but he couldn't wait to come.

Susan had lined all the little boxes she'd brought for each species with hay and tiny scraps of food. And she'd made air holes in the lids so they could breathe.

'They're so cute,' she said, 'it's like having living toys. Can I take them home with me?'

The zebras asked Susan if they could adopt her neck wrapper and marry her gloves.

I decided this was a good idea. Bert had given up on building the Noah's Ark and the squirrel incident made me think Pluke's puppies might eat the lot of them. So I said, 'Sure, but do bring them on the farm trip. I'll have to take them home after that, else Farteeta will never let me hear the end of it.'

I flew Susan back to her windowsill. 'That was the greatest night of my life,' she said. 'What a wonderful thing it is to fly.'

At home, Bert and Papa were still up, battling with the challenges of the Thregg threat. 'Have reduced Fluffy Allies suspects to six million,' Bert was saying proudly.

'Only five million, 999 thousand, 999 to eliminate then,' said Papa gloomily.

Farm trip in a few hours. With my trusty Shrinker I can capture loads of animals.

Flowk

MISSION EARTH TWO:
STILL
DAY SEVEN - WEDNESDAY

Dear Rok,

I remembered to thank Farty this morning. As I expected, she was furious I hadn't brought any animals home, but she saw the point about Pluke's puppies possibly eating them. She promised to spend the day making a safe environment and finding the right food for them.

The snow has nearly disappeared, Rok, and Earth is just its usual dull grey. I wore ludicrous welly boots for the farm trip to look like everyone else. I sat next to Susan on the coach as she had the zoo animals in her backpack.

'I'm worried they're not very comfy,' she said, 'but it's in a good cause because they'll all be free soon.'

I could hear them roaring and snuffling, but luckily their voices were too small to be within range of human hearing. I comforted Susan, saying they sounded excited, looking forward to life on Faa.

Earth countryside is very different from ours, Rok. It's mostly flat, with a scattering of trees (smaller and far less chatty than *urqflurbles*, and apparently rooted to the spot) and criss-crossed with 'fences'. Susan explained that Earthlings own different bits of their countryside. They even own trees and bushes and vegetables! It is impossible to imagine our vegetable life on Faa agreeing to be owned by anyone, but Earth vegetables are timid and barely communicate. This strange habit of dividing up the landscape means there are parts of their own planet that

Earthlings are not allowed to walk on. Perhaps they will have to buy their own air to breathe one day unless the bat brigades hurry up and take over.

When we arrived at the farm it was knee deep in a slimy substance called mud, a glopulous mixture of the planet's two main ingredients: earth and water.

'Watch out for werewolves,' said Adam One.

'And vampire bats and man-eating spiders,' said Colin.

I made a note to capture these species as Miss Barn marched us to the cowshed. The cows were bigger than lions.

'These two are called Daisy and Clover,' said Miss Barn, reading from her fact sheet. 'Scientists say that cows who have names produce more milk than cows who don't. They seem to respond to love and attention.'

'But why name us after food?' grumbled the one

called Daisy. 'How would she like to be called Sandwich?'

'Moof, my stomachs are killing me,' said Clover.

'Mine too. Been like it ever since them thistles.'

'You have more than one stomach?' I couldn't help asking quietly.

'Bull's breakfasts! You speak Bovine!' said Daisy, gazing at me from under her long eyeball lashes. She then explained at length about her digestive system, which utilises four stomach chambers to disintegrate fibrous matter, or 'grass'. If Earthlings could learn how to do this, there would be none of the ridiculous food shortages they have on their planet.

'You'll have a much better life on Faa. No more being squeezed into cow juice, or flattened into sofa covers or sharing your last moments next to a Yorkshire pudding,' I told them as I nabbed them with the Shrinker quickly when everyone else had left the shed.

I hear that on Faa there are five moons to jump over

I was delighted by the sheeps. Whenever they say a word beginning with the Earth sound 'b' they make a curious bleating sound. They do it for fun, competing to see who can make up the longest sentence. I zapped two of the cleverest sheeps with my Shrinker.

'You'll be coming to lovely Faa,' I whispered to them, 'where you will never again be woven into socks or frightened by mint sauce.'

The pigs were even more thrilled to see me than the lions had been, waddling up to the fences, snorting and chattering eagerly.

'They recognise you,' said Colin. 'Takes one to know one.'

It is unlike Colin to say something so kind, so I

thanked him, which he seemed to find very amusing.

By lunchtime, I had added goats, chickens, foxes and a couple of marvellous long-eared rabbits to my collection.

On Faa nobody will ask why I crossed the road

'Chicken' is an Earthling insult which means coward. There is very little inter-species respect.

Susan separated them all carefully, although the foxes pleaded to share with the hens and rabbits, who they said were their best friends. I believed they meant no harm, but Susan was very insistent.

Then a magical thing happened, Rok. I saw two centaurs! They were magnificent beasts, half human, half horse, just like in Earthling stories.

Susan shouted at me not to shrink them, but I had already been bossed about by her with regard to the foxes and hens, so I raced behind the pig house and aimed the Shrinker straight at the centaurs, who most alarmingly split in half. They resolved themselves into two shouting humans and two speedily shrinking creatures I recognised as Earth horses. I realised Earthlings must ride these creatures when they can't find a bicycle.

The Earthlings staggered about bellowing until a farm helper led them away. 'Yes, yes, calm down,' he told them, muttering to us, 'Someone's had one too many in the Dog and Duck.'

Luckily, I managed to find the two tiny horses, who were trying to gnaw through a now gigantic (to them) blade of grass. Susan forgave me as she was more thrilled with these than any of the other animals.

Susan loves their little 'saddles' and 'bridles' almost as much as she loves the horses.

'I've always wanted a pony,' she sighed, 'but you can't keep one in a flat. If I had one of these it could live for a year off a few sugar lumps and oats. I could ride it once a day then shrink it back and keep it in a little shoebox stable and —'

'Susan! Nigel! Hurry up!'

Miss Barn was calling us over the field to see the bull (a male cow that humans eat squashed in a bun, so in need of rescuing).

I've put all the new creatures into my coat pockets and I'm sending you this straight away, Rok. After the bull we're just going off to see farm vehicles and other boring stuff.

Space Explorer Level Ten, here I come!

Your friend in
science,
Flowk

Susan likes the idea of her horse drinking from a 'tea cup'. She has a strange Earthling imagination . . .

MISSION EARTH TWO: LATER
DAY SEVEN - WEDNESDAY

Oh Rok,

My tentacles quiver as I write. Prepare yourself for a terrible shock. I was so happy when I sent you my last message. But that wonderful day has turned into a terrible day. The worst ever.

As we hurried to catch up with the class it was starting to snowball again and Susan was complaining of the cold. Since Mama always makes me wear three coats I let her borrow my top one.

But as I was halfway across the field, Susan called me back.

'I've just seen some incredible new creatures,' she whispered. 'You can add them to your collection. Look, they're in the woods.'

I couldn't see anything but I followed Susan into a small clump of irritable trees.

'Look, aren't they gorgeous? They're like little fairy people,' she said.

I stared, horrified, at the fluffy pink creatures before us. They were not much bigger than toy teddy bears. They had huge round blue eyes, sparkly wings and sweet smiles.

It was the dreaded Wiffly Biffly.

'Come away, Susan,' I screamed, grabbing her arm. 'Come away! It is the dreaded Wiffly Biffly!'

'Don't be silly, Nigel. They're ADORABLE.'

I pulled out the Shrinker and aimed it at them, but Farteeta was right – it wasn't powerful enough for anything from outside Earth. Nothing happened and the Wiffly Biffly advanced, smiling their terrible smiles

and fluttering their twinkly wings. Susan grabbed the Shrinker from me furiously. 'Listen, they're singing.'

Sure enough, the Wiffly Biffly were humming a hypnotic song.

'We are the darling Wiffly Biffy,
we are coming softly, sniffly,
padding on our fluffy paws,
smiling with our snuffly jaws.
Sniffly wiffly! Wiffly piffly!
Grab the girly, swiftly wiftly!'

I leapt towards Susan, extending all my suckers, but there was a blinding pink flash and Susan and the Wiffly Biffly disappeared.

The ground where they had been standing was untouched – no trace of them remained, not even a footprint in the snow. It happened in a split second, and all I could hear were the dying strains of their horrible song.

'We are the gorgeous Wiffly Biffly,
we are leaving softly, swiftly.
We have your little sister-wister,
too late to moan
that you will miss her.'

I stood frozen with fear, as a slip of paper fluttered down among the snowballs. On it were these words.

Bring us the entire
Earth's supply of
blatkerzoopyfloom,
known to humans as
CARDBOARD,
or else she dies.
We will roast her on a slow
spit and eat her with
meringues and jellied eels
on Saturday morning.
Oh, and Keith says your
planet will soon be just a
spinach garden.

I heard a distant laugh, 'HAR HAR HOO.' The unmistakable cackling of Keith, King of Threggs.

'Susan! Susan!' I screamed. My unhappy head shot out of my coats, followed closely by my worried head and my philosophical head. My happy head sprang after them, weeping like it has never done before. I don't know how I got my one Earth head to remember to take some *Vom*, but luckily I did, so that all my other heads had retracted just as Miss Barn panted over the field.

'Whatever's the matter, Nigel?'

'Susan has been kidnapped by aliens!' I wailed.

'I'm sure she's just hiding,' said Miss Barn. 'Susan, come out now, you're being a silly girl. You've frightened Nigel. Come on out.'

But there was no sound except a faint wind in the trees and an even fainter laugh. 'HAR HAR HOO.'

We searched for Susan for half an hour before Miss Barn phoned the police.

Shrieking cars arrived and officers surged out shouting into radios. Two policemen, PC Wheedle and PC Barge, asked me lots of questions. I told them the truth, Rok, but they didn't believe me.

'Aliens, you say?' said PC Barge. 'Fluffy pink ones? That's original.'

I began to worry they thought I had kidnapped Susan and looked to Miss Barn for help.

'He wouldn't have harmed her, Constable,' said Miss Barn. 'They're good friends. I think Susan must have run away. Perhaps she's in trouble at home.'

'Lots of alien rumours flying around this week,' said PC Barge, patting my hairstyle and closing one eye in such an extreme way I thought some insect must have flown in until I realised it was an Earth 'wink'.

'Two-headed puppies, children flying into

planes. I expect young Nigel here has been reading too many newspapers. Don't worry, sonny,
we'll find your friend,' he added kindly, because
my Earth eyeballs were by now crying tears of
sheer frustration. How I would have loved to throw
off my disguise and show them the whole truth.
But I knew that wouldn't help find Susan. I knew
the only people who could help Susan were we
Faathings, brave and true.

Jatinder, Annie Spratt, Ben Bingle and even Adams
One and Two were wailing all the way back on the
school bus. Everyone kept handing each other bogey
tissues, which seemed most unhygienic. Even Colin
Snell was quiet. Roddy was crying hardest of all. He
said Susan was the only person who talked to him
apart from me. Miss Barn told us school would be
closed for the rest of the week, but she was sure the
police would find Susan 'in no time', as if such a
thing were possible.

* * *

'The Wiffly Biffly are here!' I shouted as I tore into our hallway.

'What?!' Papa looped from his chair, his worried head shooting out of his jacket.

'They've kidnapped her! They will EAT her!'

'What are you talking about? Farteeta's safe in her room. Isn't she?'

Papa and Mama zoomed upstairs and came down with Farty.

'How dare you frighten us like that!' shouted Papa.

'Not Farty, Susan! They've kidnapped Susan!'

Papa relaxed. 'Well, that's all right then. That means they've mistaken her for Farteeta. Are you certain it was the Wiffly Biffly? How big were they?'

'Tiny, but terrifying.'

'Hmm,' said Papa, absent-mindedly scanning Bert's list of dangerous fluffy species. 'Did they ask for a ransom?'

'Yes. The entire world's supply of cardboard. By Saturday.'

'Excellent. That's very good news. They won't bother us before that, and we'll have gone by then. All the milkman's friends will be Improved on Friday, so we can leave for Faa straight after. Don't worry about it,' he added kindly, ruffling my hairstyle.

'Don't worry about it? Susan's my friend. She's a person.'

Papa sighed. 'This sometimes happens to us when we explore other planets, Flowkwee. We Faathings can grow fond of inferior species. I understand you care for Susan as you would for a favourite pet, but we Faathings must be brave and true and not always listen to our hearts. In the end, Susan is only a feeble Earthling.'

Papa thrust his Earth population calculator under my beak. 'Look

how many of them there are. Three hundred and two Earthlings have been born just in the minute we've been talking. No one will miss Susan.'

'But I will miss her,' I said.

'No darling,' said Mama. 'You will be happy on Faa, playing *fatool* and seeing your real friends again. You'll forget all about Susan.'

'But what about her mum? Adult Earthlings might have *some* feelings . . .'

At this, Mama's sad face emerged briefly from her left shoulder but she sipped some *Vom*, smiled a big Earthling smile and said, 'Susan's mum will probably be quite pleased. She's a busy person driving her bus, and Earthling children are a lot of work, especially for just one mummy.'

'Really?' I asked, hoping it was true. I felt I needed to change the subject so I asked, 'What will the Wiffly Biffly do when they arrive here and we've gone?'

'They'll probably eat Susan first,' said Papa. 'Then

they'll seek out all the cardboard. When they've taken every box and tube and package they'll make the Earthlings turn all the woods and forests into cardboard. Then they'll take the cardboard and eat the Earthlings. After that, the Threggs will come and cultivate Earth into a vast spinach plantation. But you needn't worry about that, Flowkwee, because they can't hurt us. We'll be gone by then.'

'Don't you care about Earth at all?' I asked.

'A little, of course. It's sad when a planet's ruined, but we will have saved a few hundred Earthlings and all your creatures.'

And that's when I realised.

'Oh no! Susan's got all my animals with her. I lent her my coat. She's got half of them in her backpack and half in the pockets of my coat.'

'WHAT?! Why didn't you tell us in the first place?' Papa shouted. But he calmed down quite quickly. 'It can't be helped now. You'd better just

take flies and mice and that poodle creature next door then. And some pigeons. Really, Flowkwee, you are *hopeless*. I don't know why I entrusted you with this Mission in the first place. We're off back to Faa on Friday, like it or not.'

I have failed. Papa no longer admires me. My Mission is over. I will never hold my heads up again if I return to Faa with only pigeons and a poodle.

What do you think about Susan?

On the one gripper, I want to believe Papa and Mama. On another gripper, Miss Barn looked unhappy about Susan so I expect Susan's mum will be unhappy too. As you know, another example of Earthlings' primitive development is that they only have one mum, but perhaps they do as much caring as our four or five mothers do.

Your confused friend,
Flowk

MISSION EARTH TWO: DAY EIGHT - THURSDAY

Dear Rok,

I woke up at midnight with all of Pluke's puppies snoring on my head, and my messager bleeping. It was great to get your reply. Fantastic news about the *fatool* scores. I knew those *fnurfling* Pyez would lose the next seventeen games. And it's nice of you to say I shouldn't worry too much about Susan. Perhaps you are right that she eats creatures, so why shouldn't she get eaten herself? But I have to follow my feelings, Rok, and do my best to save her some-how. I said so to Farty, who was reading the

Encyclopedia of Predators, finding out all she could about the Wiffly Biffly.

'What's the point?' she said. 'Papa's right, there are plenty more Earthlings.'

'But what about my creatures? The Emperor could vaporise me for failure.'

'Good point,' she said. 'To rescue your creatures in time for us to take them to Faa, we need the Wiffly Biffly to arrive before Papa's Improved everyone. If we can collect enough cardboard, hopefully the Wiffly Biffly will be attracted to it and come earlier than expected. Then we can rescue the animals – and Susan too, if you really want – and obliterate the Wiffly Biffly.'

'But what with?'

'Custard, of course.'

Luckily Mama has been doing a thing called 'bulk buying' to make us look more like Earthlings. The kitchen had forty-eight tins of custard, fifty-six cereal packets and two hundred toilet rolls.

Farty and me conquered our disgust and unrolled all the toilet rolls in my bedroom so we could get at the cardboard tubes in the middle. Pluke's puppies loved it, romping around like an advertisement. We assembled all the cereal packets, and the big boxes that the TV and tarantula pictures had come in and we sneaked outside and piled them out of sight behind the shed.

But even two hundred toilet rolls, fifty-six cereal boxes and a few big boxes is not

very much cardboard, Rok. Our pile looked pathetic and small – nothing like a big enough supply to attract the Wiffly Biffly. Worse, Mama went mental when she saw us taking the custard tins to set our trap.

'I need that custard to make pies for the milkman and his friends!'

'We need reinforcements,' whispered Farty.

I texted Roddy, Orville Muffin and Aaron Ratchett.

EMERGENCY. S.O.S. SAVE OUR SUSAN. SHE CAN ONLY BE SAVED BY CARDBOARD. BRING LOTS TO MY HOUSE. PASS IT ON.

'Did you mention the custard? We'll need loads,' said Farteeta.

I keyed in *P.S. AND BRING LOTS OF CUSTARD!*

'That's the best we can do for now,' said Farteeta.

I'd have flown off to hunt for cardboard and

custard, but Bert put his foot down. 'Wiffly might realise Susan is Earthling and come back for you. Orders are to stay within dwelling.'

The rest of the day went very slowly, Rok. I couldn't help thinking about where Susan was, if the Wiffly Biffly were being horrible to her, if she was frightened and wanted her mummy – or maybe even me. And knowing the feebleness of Earthlings, I didn't have much hope my friends would really come and help. Me and Farteeta would have to try our best, with the one tin of custard we'd managed to keep, and hope our small pile of cardboard would be enough to tempt the Wiffly Biffly so we could rescue Susan.

Mama spent the time zooming about the kitchen making Marmite and cauliflower snacks and infuriatingly wasting the custard by cooking it in pies mixed with cabbage and teabags, while

Papa and Bert were in the shed making last minute adjustments to the Improver.

I have just swigged a triple dose of *Vom*, Papa's advice in case the Improver event of tomorrow gets too exciting and our disguises dissolve. If the Improver *does* work and we capture hundreds of slaves and escape before the Wiffly Biffly arrive, I will have failed in my Mission. And Susan will have been eaten.

Your unhappy friend,

Flowk

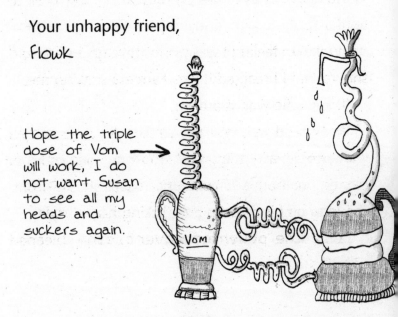

Hope the triple dose of Vom will work, I do not want Susan to see all my heads and suckers again.

MISSION EARTH TWO: DAY NINE - FRIDAY

Hi Rok,

Things have moved on pretty fast. I can't wait to tell you.

I woke up feeling I was flying through an asteroid shower until I realised it was Farteeta shaking me.

'Look!' she was shouting.

We looked out into the street. It was crammed with people, all jostling and elbowing each other to get to our house. The milkman was at the front, showing off his muscles and flicking his hairstyle.

'**It's the power of advertising,**' bleeped

Bert, whizzing into the room looking very pleased with himself – as much as anything can with only a blue plastic globe and a set of coloured lights for a head. 'Earthling emotions regarding appearance-improvement engaged by massive leafleting campaign.'

'How in the name of Flinghuuurn's *flimunious* hammer will the Improver cope with all that lot?' asked Farteeta.

'My Improver can cope with anything!' Bert squeaked triumphantly. 'Major performance upgrade solution now complete! Mission activated!'

We ran downstairs to see Mama had gone over the top, as usual. She had followed Papa's advice to dress smartly so she had a lot of red paint on her mouth and cheeks and was wearing a long skirt and cloak which dragged on the ground, shiny necklaces and a spiky hat covered in sparkles.

'Do step this way for your exhilarating Health Club and Beauty Parlour experience,' she was shouting, offering the crowd custard and teabag pies, loaves crammed with pasta and mugs of boiling whisky with straws. 'Weight reducing for the ladies and furry heads and excellent fat muscles for the gents.'

Papa stood by the shed door. 'Step this way, please,' he said. 'First, can we have two ladies who wish to lose weight?'

Twenty-four enormous females crowded up.

'You will all get your turn,' he said, winking at me.

Papa chose two fat ladies, and two more ladies who wanted bigger chest bumps, then two weedy men who wanted muscles and two bald men who wanted hairstyles.

Everyone else stood waiting excitedly in the living room, laughing rudely at Mama's nice pictures and little knowing that when their turn came they were going to be made into slaves.

The Improver shimmered and shook. I had lost faith in it by now, Rok, and expected the worst.

Sure enough the two huge females came out as round as before, but floated into the air like gas balloons.

'Eek, harooh, yoweee,' they squealed.

Everyone raced outside just in time to see them soaring out of reach. They hovered above the trees, bobbing in the breeze and wailing.

'They've lost weight all right, but not fat,' said a voice from the crowd, and several people started laughing. But one small male with a white hairstyle shouted, 'Brenda, my beloved, come back, come back. I love you just the way you are, my little plumpyness!'

'As you can see, it's a powerful machine,' said Papa, fiddling with the controls. 'Just a few minor adjustments needed.' However, the mood changed when the next victims emerged: the chest bumps women had grown fur on their legs, the bald men grew extra legs and were covered in fur except for their heads, and the men who wanted muscles had grown them on their beaks, ears and necks.

'You've turned us into monsters!' they shouted, sounding very angry and upset.

'You look much better to me,' Papa said, 'but if you're not happy, it's easily reversible – just pop back in.'

'He's right,' said our friend the milkman. 'It went a bit funny on me the first time I tried it, but look at me now.'

He rolled up his sleeve to demonstrate his handsome muscles and a female hanging on his arm said, 'Yes, he's twice the man he was. Give it another go.'

The furry-legged females and bald males were about to stumble grumbling back into the Improver when a lot of yelling and shouting distracted them. There was another noisy crowd heading up the street, Rok – smaller Earthlings, but just as many of them. This time it was my entire class, plus a whole bunch of other children I didn't even recognise, carrying armfuls and bags of cardboard. Orville Muffin had even brought his tiny dog. You couldn't normally tell its front and back end apart, but this time the big cardboard box of Warthog's Choccoblasters it was carrying in its mouth gave the game away.

'Sorry we didn't come by yesterday, Nigel,' said Orville. 'It took us ages to collect all this cardboard. How's it going to help find Susan?'

I was just thinking what to say when Orville Muffin's dog, Choccoblasters and all, shot into the Improver before anyone could stop it – and fast out the other end, ten times its size, completely bald except for a human beard, and with huge, pointy fangs. They would have made it look very fierce, except it still had the same mad but quite friendly smile, very much like Orville's.

'Awesome,' said Orville, distracted. 'I've always wanted a bigger dog.'

The Choccoblasters packet hadn't changed much, except in one quite important way. It was

growing at a phenomenal rate when it came out of the Improver and was soon about three times the height of our house, like a cardboard mountain. We looked up, and the two Balloon Women were perched on the top of it, their little legs dangling over the lid.

'Saved!' cried Brenda's little male. 'Somebody get a ladder and rescue my plumpy dumpling.'

Then we heard it. A telltale sound, gentle at first but getting louder, until it was clear enough for even the Earthlings to hear.

'We are the dreaded Wiffly Biffly
with our smiles so squiffly wiffly
and our little wings so sparkly
through deep space so darkly quarkly.
Here's our leader, Woffly Boffly,
licks his lips so scoffly quaffly,
he must never be ignored,
no galaxy left unexplored
in our quest for our adored
CARDBOARD.'

Everyone looked up and there were luminous pink circular spacecrafts gathering in the sky.

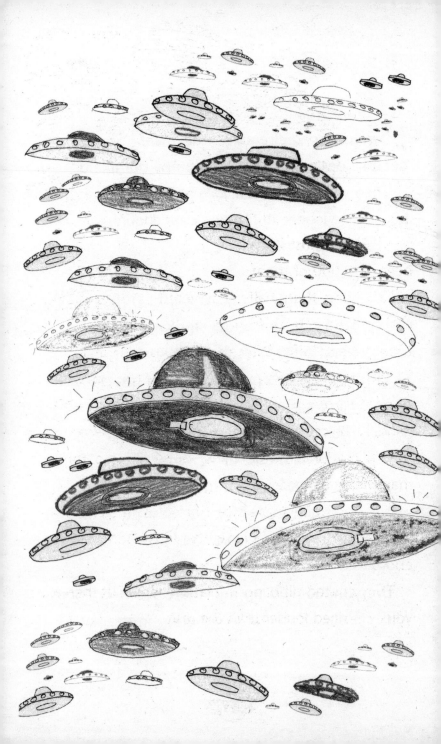

There must have
been 200,000 of them.

Each one then halted, hovered
and opened a hatch from which poured
thousands of Wiffly Biffly, till the sky turned pink.

'Oh no,' said Papa, staring at the massive
Choccoblasters box before putting his face in his
hands. 'The cardboard must have brought them.'

'What adorable little birds,' squealed the milkman's female friend.

But her smile turned to horror as about forty
Wiffly Biffly surged towards the fat floating ladies
and bared their razor sharp fangs.

They started nibbling the ladies' legs. But then a
voice boomed louder than the rest:

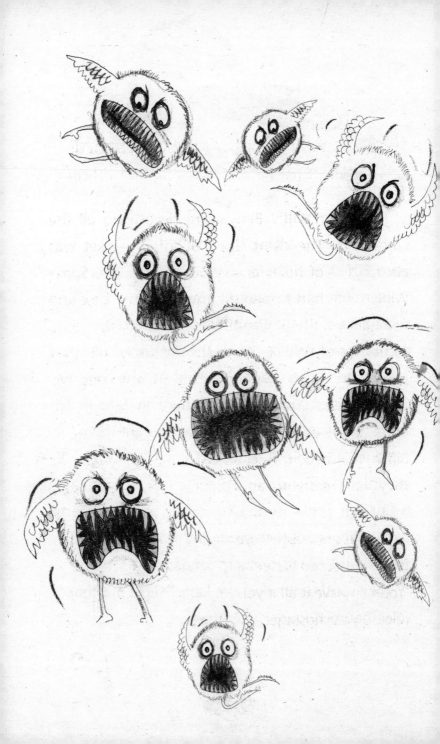

'No snacking! Collect the cardboard!
We can eat the Earthling fatties later.'

The other Wiffly Biffly were destroying all the cardboard. The giant Choccoblasters packet was already full of holes and about to collapse. Some Wiffly Biffly had ripped off chunks of the box and were kissing them, some were dancing with them, some were talking to them heatedly till they caught fire, others were cuddling them to bits. My class were yelling and waving their arms about as swooping Wiffly Biffly grabbed the cardboard they were carrying and made off with it.

'We've got loads more cardboard,' shouted Farteeta. 'You can have it all if you release your hostage.'

'Why should we?'

'Because you said you would.'

'Oh no we didn't.'

'OH YES YOU DID.'

'DIDN'T!'

'DID!'

Farteeta shrugged. 'They've got no morals. Get the custard, it's our only hope.'

'Where's the custard?' I asked Orville and Jatinder.

'What custard?' they said.

They didn't bring any. I must have forgotten to send my second text. No custard. We are doomed.

I'm sending you this from my bedroom, where I'm collecting the one measly tin of custard that me and Farteeta saved, as if that could possibly do any good. It's unlikely you'll hear from me again.

Love to all my mothers.

Flowk

MISSION EARTH TWO: STILL DAY NINE – FRIDAY

Rok,

After I sent you my last message, I decided I had to do my best to rescue Susan, no matter just how impossible it seemed. I tore back into the garden, clutching my custard tin.

'YOU'RE ALL LIARS, CHEATS WHO DON'T KEEP THEIR PROMISES, AND WEEDY PINK THINGS!' I shouted up at the pink Wiffly-infected sky.

'You tell 'em, Nigel,' said Orville Muffin. There was a chorus of agreement from the rest of the class.

'I demand to see the hostage,' I said.

'Oh all right then. Here she is,'
said a voice coming from the inside of the leading
spacecraft, that made all the other Wiffly Biffly go
quiet. The flying spacecraft swooped down. A
second hatch opened revealing Susan, tied to a
stake.

'As you see, we have invited her for tea.
And she is to be the tea, roasted
with meringues and jellied eels,
unless you give over the entire
world's supply of cardboard
by midnight tonight.'

We all gasped in horror. Susan held her chin up
bravely. Then something amazing happened.

First there was a squeak, then a trumpet, then a
hiss, then a roar. Susan's backpack started to expand.
It wobbled and wriggled as though it had come

alive. The effects of the Shrinker were wearing off. The zoo animals were growing back to normal size!

Startled by Susan's sudden expansion, the Wiffly Biffly were caught off guard. It seemed like the moment for my best *fatool* moves, before the creatures reached full size. So I sprang from the ground and climbed steeply, extending three tentacles to wrap around Susan, dived left to avoid an undaunted squadron of Wiffly Biffly, turned sharply and landed next to my cheering class just as the backpack was getting too big for even my tentacles to envelop. A small tiger's head appeared, then an elephant's, then a giraffe's on the end of its long neck. And then Susan's coat seemed to explode! Although we had shrunk the zoo animals a few hours before the farm ones, they now seemed to be expanding too at almost the same rate, because soon the cows and sheeps and pigs appeared. They flopped out of Susan's pockets

about the size of kittens to start with, then they grew back to their proper sizes at tremendous speed.

The tiger growled, showing massive fangs. The giraffe wondered whether to eat the Snells' TV aerial and then decided against it.

Annie Spratt surprised us all by jumping on a horse's back and galloping round the garden, going, 'Woo-hoo, always wanted to do this!' Unfortunately the horse ran straight into the Improver with a frightening sound of whinnying and wailing.

The class all squealed as something that was half horse, half Annie came hurtling out of the ejector chute. A gorgon hairstyle clipping that I now realised was called a 'snake' wound itself around the milkman's friend's leg, and she screamed so that me and Farteeta jumped about an Earth metre in the air. I have never been so relieved we all took extra *Vom*.

But then the voice spoke again:

'Revenge for rescuing hostage follows swiftly after cardboard break.
Don't go away.
You will all be snacks soon.'

The Wiffly Biffly went back to nuzzling and hugging the cardboard. They certainly *did* like cardboard. Everyone was scared, waiting to see what the Wiffly Biffly would do once they'd had their break.

The garden was crammed with full-size wolves growling at orang-utans, meerkats rearing up at prickly porcupines, sheeps and chickens hiding behind trees, cows moaning about their indigestion, elephants trumpeting at lions, fat furry Earthling Improver-specimens running about yelling, eagles swooping on Wiffly Biffly and veering away at the sight of their razor fangs, and penguins staring up at the pink horde above and falling over on their backs.

'Oh no,' Susan said, clutching me. 'Who's going to eat us first, the animals or the Wiffly Biffly?'

Papa was issuing instructions in all directions, and Mama was nodding agreement, but nobody was taking any notice of either of them. It was painful to watch, Rok, but there's a time when you realise your parents don't control everything.

Above it all I could hear a yapping that signalled the arrival of Pluke's puppies and the bleeping of the fearless Bert. Their appearance immediately spooked the animals (even though robots and two-headed puppies look pretty normal to us) who all backed away snarling, crawling over each other, and thrashing around. Darren the lion almost pushed me into the compost heap in his hurry to get out of the way.

'Sorry, mate,' he said to me, 'but this is terrible.

We were better off in the zoo. First it's a lot of pink birds that look like snacks and turn out to have sharper teeth than the missus, then it's monsters with too many legs and giants with flashing lights. I'm too old for this game.'

Trying to scare off an approaching elephant, Colin Snell grabbed my only tin of custard and threw it at its head. It just bounced off and the elephant stepped on it, squirting a jet of custard into the air.

Its effect, Rok, was astounding.

The Wiffly Biffly instantly stopped nuzzling cardboard and froze, their eyeballs swivelling anxiously. Some of them were already shivering.

Then I remembered Mama's custard and teabag pies, which the Earthlings had rudely refused to eat. 'Get the pies!' I shouted as I quickly grabbed the squashed tin from under the elephant's feet. Roddy, Aaron Ratchett and Jatinder raced out with armfuls of custard pies which they pelted at the Wiffly Biffly.

But they weren't like the custard pies in the old film. They had gone cold and solid and only seemed to give the Wiffly Biffly the faintest hint of shame.

I showed Farteeta the custard tin. It still had about two millilitres of custard glooping about inside.

'Can we expand it?' I was desperate now.

'You bet,' she said, carrying the tin to the Improver as though it was the most valuable thing in the Universe. Which it was.

The Wiffly Biffly were regrouping for their final attack . . .

'Here we come so pinkly winkly
coming faster than
you thinkly
with our mouths so
dribbly wibbly

and our fangs so wibbly nibbly.
He who laughs at Wiffly Biffly
sees his doom and sees it swiftly.'

The Improver enlarged the custard. It gushed out
of the ejector chute, quickly turning the garden into
a sticky yellow pond. The elephant sucked the
custard up, firing a stream of it at a cluster of Wiffly
Biffly. In an instant they were bald and quivering.

'Cowardy cowardy custard,' yelled Farteeta.

To see the custard hit the
Wiffly Biffly, move the page
towards you until your beak
touches the planet.

'Who dares to call us custard?'

When they heard this single voice, all the Wiffly Biffly bowed down, chanting:

'Master of all he surveys, Lord of Lords,
Bunoon of Bunoons, Wiffly of Bifflies.
Tremble in terror, be very very dismayed,
for you have made him very angry.
It is he! Highest of the most high.
Biggest of the most big,
enormous of the
most enormous,
HIS ROYAL VASTNESS.'

A gold platform with twiddly bits shot out of the leading spacecraft's hatch. A tiny pink fluffy creature wearing medals and a peaked cap stepped out onto the platform, and squeaked:

'I am Woffly Boffly,
leader of the Wiffly Biffly
from the planet Boffly Woffly!'

It began with a giggle from Orville, Jatinder and Aaron, grew to a chuckle and exploded into a gale of laughter as others joined in. Soon everyone was falling about in hysterics.

Woffly Boffly tried to puff himself up but then deflated.

'Who dares insult Woffly Boffly?!
We have banned humour
from the Universe!
Go away! Stop it!'

He put his wings over his ears, but the laughing grew louder and louder.

'That's it, of course. They hate laughter!' said Farteeta, jumping up and down excitedly.

The Wiffly Biffly started to shrink, their pinkness growing paler and paler, until they fell into the custard lake, as shrivelled as dead leaves.

A second later, any remaining Wiffly Biffly fled into their spacecraft.

The voice of Woffly Boffly could just be heard above the roaring of the animals.

'Keith, you've really landed us in it.
You never told me
they had custard,
and worse, they LAUGH.'

'He's talking to Keith, King of Threggs,' whispered Farteeta.

'Oh don't worry about Keith,' said Susan. 'He's scared of music. He's probably even frightened of nursery rhymes.'

And, as suddenly as they had appeared, all the pink spacecraft vanished. The sky cleared. A huge cheer went up from the crowd.

'You'll never defeat us,' Susan shouted at the sky. 'Not as long as we have music. And jokes!'

And, in the now clear sky, we could see our own familiar spaceship with Flyzoop at the controls. We could also hear approaching sirens.

'Earthling police,' bleeped Bert. 'Mission

aborted. Can't take creatures to Faa. Must shrink them first. Unsafe travelling companions at that size.'

Susan was fishing frantically in the pockets of my coat. Thank *Klong* she still had the Shrinker, which she'd snatched during the fateful farm trip.

It took seconds to shrink the creatures, Rok, so I have lots to bring back to Faa. Papa wasn't so lucky. We managed to reverse the Improver successfully to make all the victims look normal again (at least, as normal as Earthlings can ever look), but we didn't have time to hang around and Improve any of them.

We memory blasted all the Earthlings, who said they'd had a lovely time and were happy just the way they were after all, while Susan and Roddy helped me collect up all the tiny animals.

As Flyzoop came in to land, I noticed Annie Spratt, still half girl, half horse, nibbling some grass behind the shed. Farteeta suggested I shrink her and bring her home.

'Isn't that the centaur you've always wanted?' she asked.

'How dare you!' said Susan. 'I thought you had feelings, because you bothered to rescue me. But you only cared about getting the animals, didn't you? And now you're thinking of murdering Annie.'

'It's not murder,' I protested. 'Look how happy she is as a centaur. She was always crying before.'

. . . to see happy Annie Spratt in her woolly hat

Turn the horse upside-down . . .

'Reverse her, now, you beast!'

I didn't like Susan calling me a beast, so we let the Annie creature go and thankfully the Improver spat her out in the right pieces.

'Best fun I've had in years,' Annie said as we memory blasted her.

'Susan, you know I do like you,' I said to her when Annie was back to normal. 'It's just that we Faathings have more complex brains than Earthlings, and —'

'Thanks very much,' she said huffily.

Flyzoop landed seconds later and we let all the little animals gallop into the spacecraft. Pluke, his puppies and Fi Fi next door followed. I turned to see if I could persuade Susan to come with us, but I was already changing back into my Faathing form. She shivered and drew away.

'I'm sorry, Nigel, you just can't be my friend when you look like that.'

'But *you* are *my* friend! And you look hideous to me,' I said without thinking.

'Oh. Is that how you feel?' she said, turning her back on me.

'I've got a present for you,' I told her. 'You can share it with Annie and Roddy.' She looked round.

I gave her one of the tiny horses. And the Shrinker.

'We won't need it on Faa,' I said.

The look on Susan's face made my hearts expand so much I thought they'd burst, but Flyzoop was screaming at us to hurry and Bert bundled everyone into the spacecraft just as the police cars and ambulances arrived outside our house.

'Don't forget me, Susan. I'll always be your friend. And yours too, Roddy,' I shouted, as the anti-matter shield encircled us, making us invisible.

My last memory of Earth is a blurry image of Susan and Roddy, waving blankly at the empty sky. Susan was holding her tiny horse. I think the image was blurry because I may have been crying, Rok. How odd.

'It's peculiar, isn't it,' I said to Farteeta as we settled into the spacecraft's comfort zone, 'that Earthlings, who are so dumb, have discovered two things we never have: music and jokes? And these two things are strong enough to defeat the two most evil species in the Universe.'

'Mmmm,' said Farteeta. 'I suppose there is some-thing in that.'

And I'm sure I heard a distant voice saying,

'HOO HAR.
THAT'S WHAT YOU THINK.
WE'LL BE BACK.
WIFFLY BIFFLY ARE WEEDY SCUM.
THE THREGGS' NEXT ALLIES
WILL DESTROY YOU
TO OBLIVION.'

So that's it for now, Rok. We're hurtling towards you safe and sound, and Papa and Bert think the Emperor will be so impressed with all my creatures that he'll forgive us for not having any human slaves. But I am not so sure.

Can't wait to see you, old friend. It's been a busy week.

Flowk

Is this a puzzle?
(Turn it upside down)

For out of this world activities,
a Faarthing guide,
and to read Flowkwee's
galactic blog,
go to:

www.alienschoolboy.co.uk

Look out for the next
Letters from
an Alien
Schoolboy
book:

Galactic
Poodle

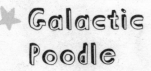